Land of the Cold Sky

Shane McQuaid Series

Bruce Dunavin & Jim C. Jennings

WestBow
PRESS
A DIVISION OF THOMAS NELSON

WestBow Press books may be ordered through booksellers or by contacting:

WestBow Press
A Division of Thomas Nelson
1663 Liberty Drive
Bloomington, IN 47403
www.westbowpress.com
1-(866) 928-1240

Because of the dynamic nature of the Internet, any web addresses or links contained in this book may have changed since publication and may no longer be valid. The views expressed in this work are solely those of the author and do not necessarily reflect the views of the publisher, and the publisher hereby disclaims any responsibility for them.

Any people depicted in stock imagery provided by Thinkstock are models, and such images are being used for illustrative purposes only.

Certain stock imagery © Thinkstock.

ISBN: 978-1-4497-7290-1 (s)
ISBN: 978-1-4497-7289-5 (hc)
ISBN: 978-1-4497-7288-8 (e)

Library of Congress Control Number: 2012923039

Printed in the United States of America

WestBow Press rev. date: 12/28/2012

Dedication

I dedicate this book to Steve Englert, a true mountain man!

Bruce Dunavin

To Donna, my wife and best friend, without whom I would be in a whole lot of trouble with God!

Jim Jennings

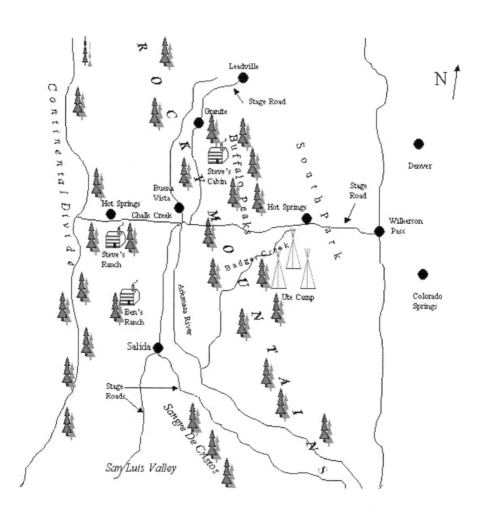

Introduction

THE BLACK HORSE

Jed Parker was a strange man, least that's what some folks thought. Even at the ripe old age of 70, his lined, sun-darkened face looked like cracked mud in a dried-up creek, Jed was as spry as a spring colt and his reflexes had not slowed very much either. His beloved wife having passed away several years back, he kept mostly to himself. He much preferred the company of horses to people. Now, if there was one thing that could be said about Ol' Jed, it was his unusual ability with animals, especially horses. If you wanted a quality-bred horse that could work, run, or last all day, you went to Jed Parker. Folks came from far and wide to deal with Jed. But some went away disappointed. The reason was simple, if Jed didn't take to ya, you were out of luck doing any kind of business with him and no amount of pleading or dinero would change his mind. You had to go to him, make a request, and Jed would, likely as not, tell you to come back tomorrow and he'd have an answer. What people didn't know was Jed always prayed and sought the Lord's opinion about doing business with someone. Jed's final decision was never wrong because God was never wrong. As far as Jed was concerned, if God said it, that was it and if you didn't like it tough luck. Take your business someplace else! There were those who didn't take to the way Jed did business. They called him all kind of names; the one most used was Ol' Coot! Didn't bother Jed a bit, because those who knew and called him friend recognized an inner peace that many envied. Get in a discussion with Jed and sooner or later, the conversation would shift from horses to matters of the soul and where you would wind up when you died. There were those, now deceased, if they could talk, would have thanked Jed for those conversations.

As usual, when spring rolled around it was breeding time. Jed did what he always did...check with 'Tha Boss' to see what He preferred. This time what Jed heard was a real head scratcher. A combination he would not have ordinarily chosen. The stallion was a brute of a horse, black as hard coal, strong legged, muscles rippling with each stride. His neck was massive with a long flowing mane and tail. He had an exceptional alertness and quickness in spite of his size. He also had an attitude that said, "Don't mess with me"! He stood eighteen hands high and was named Sanhedrin, Sam for short. The horse was more wild than tame and Jed couldn't remember why he kept him around.

The brood mare, on the other hand, was one of Jed's favorites. Her coat was copper colored and shined like a new penny. She was long legged, strong of limb, quick witted and gentle natured... if she liked you. She stood a graceful fifteen and a half hands high. Her name was Rose of Shannon – Rose for short

Jed had learned from experience to trust and obey what the Lord told him to do. Therefore, when it came time to mate the pair, Jed turned the mare out into the fenced paddock. Rose took one look at the stallion and definitely didn't want to play. She wanted nothing to do with this giant of a horse that seemed intent on doing her bodily harm. What ensued was a lot of running, chasing and in general bad temper on the part of the brood mare. Jed was beginning to wonder if he had made a mistake, when all of a sudden, Rose settled down pretty as you please and allowed Sanhedrin to mate with her as if nothing had ever been wrong. "Just like a woman to change her mind," Jed thought as he watched the pair getting to know each other.

When it came time for the mare to foal, everyone was excited to see what would be the result of the unusual breeding. From the time the foal could stand, she had a mind of her own. As the weeks turned into months, the months into one year and then two it was obvious to Jed the foal was special. There was something different about her in comparison to the other new foals. Jed had trained many fine horses but never one like Lady of Sanhedrin. 'Lady' for short. It was as though Lady trained him. Jed never prayed so much over one horse, not so much for her but for himself; that he would know how to nurture this great filly and ultimately what to do with her. There were plenty of folks that put forth all manner of suggestions, most dealing with racing but Jed remained non-committal. It seemed there was a special destiny for this filly that loved to run. Jed wanted God's wisdom before he made any decision on the disposition of this special foal, in spite of all the hoop-ta-la.

One hot, summer morning, at the start of the filly's third year, Jed was sitting at his office desk tending to business when he thought he heard a buggy drive by. He looked out the desk window but saw nothing. Still he knew he had heard something so he walked out the front door and looked toward the exercise paddock. That's when he saw two men getting out of a fancy buggy that had stopped by the corral. The one on the right, smoking a large cheroot, was a big man, well dressed with an air of authority about him. The other was of medium height, stocky built and appeared to be of a lesser caliber. Jed wasn't expecting anybody so he took his gun belt off the peg by the front door and strapped it on before exiting the house.

The two strangers were looking at the horses that Jed turned out earlier to get exercise. As Jed neared the corral, he had a feeling something was not quite right. He loosened the leather hammer loop of his 44 Colt just in case he needed it, fast!

"Howdy, can I help ya," he said as he approached the two men.

Hearing Jed, both turned and Jed knew his initial premonition had been right. These two galoots weren't horse people. As the big man turned, discarding his cigar in the dirt, a slow shallow smile played across his face. He had lifeless eyes set in a hard, even cruel face. Jed's right hand casually went to his gun butt and rested there. The eyes of the other stranger, whom Jed noticed had an ugly scar on his right cheek, didn't miss the move. The big man smiled again, extending his hand, and said, "Mr. Parker I presume?"

"Yep, that's my name, who might you two be?" Jed didn't shake the man's hand.

As the man withdrew his hand it turned into a fist before it relaxed.

"My name is Smith. I want to buy that black filly over there."

"She ain't fer sale just yet. I ain't finished with her trainin'. Besides that, I ain't sure just what I plan ta' do with 'er yet. You'll have to come back in about a year or so. Next time, be sure to send me a telegram afore ya come." Not once did Jed take his eyes off either man. The big man stiffened but kept his composure.

"I am prepared to offer you twice, in cash, what the going price for such a horse is."

"I don't think you quite understood me Mister. The filly ain't fer sale. In fact she ain't fer sale to you now or anytime, now git! Jed nodded toward the other stranger, "And take him with ya!"

The man made a move forward but was stopped by Smith's right arm and a look that said "Not now!" "Well, I'm sorry you feel that way," Smith said. With that, both men got back in their fancy buggy, turned around and left, leaving a cloud of dust as they went.

As they rode away, the big man, whose name was not Smith but Lou Blonger turned, and in a voice seething with rage, said, "See to it that you take care of the matter quietly and quickly."

"Yes boss, I'll see ta it personally," he rasped, as an evil grin spread across his scarred face. "Where you want me ta take the horse?"

"Bring her late at night to the old barn on the east side of town. Be sure no one sees you."

"You know me boss, quiet as a mouse with socks on."

"See that you are." With that, he lit a fresh cheroot, leaned back and enjoyed the ride back to town. His associate, however, was deep in thought, a sardonic grin spreading across his face.

As Jed watched them leave, he knew he might not have seen the last of those two. "Well, we'll be ready fer um by golly," he thought. Little did Jed know the true nature of the man he had just talked to.

Chapter 1

Arrival at Last!

1866 Colorado Territory

"Those must be the Rocky Mountains," Roy said excitedly to Kate. "Shane, come up here and look at the mountains you've been pesterin' me about.

Shane poked his head out from the covered wagon and said, "I don't see any mountains."

"Look way out there toward the west as far as you can see," said his father.

"Oh, you mean that jagged purple line and that taller hill in the middle?"

"Yep, said Roy, "That must be Pike's Peak.

"Whoopee!" shouted Shane.

It was over three long months of hearing "when are we gonna get there Dad?" They had been nearly sixty miles out when they first saw Pikes Peak. This was something they just were not prepared for. These Rocky Mountains were far in excess of anything they were expecting to see. Pikes Peak loomed over Colorado Springs like an enormous stone fortress.

The town was built right up next to the foothills of the Rockies. Shane thought it was the most beautiful place he had ever seen.

1

"Dad, why would anyone live in flat St. Louis when they could live here?"

His dad laughed, "I was just wonderin' the same thing son."

Roy pulled up in front of a general store. The sign over the door read Seth Hoier - Proprietor. They all climbed down from the wagon and walked up the stone steps into the well-stocked store.

"Howdy," sounded a deep but friendly voice from behind a counter. The speaker was a big man with a full beard wearing a leather apron and holding a broom. There were tobacco stains all down the front of his shirt. Ain't seen ya round these parts afore. The name's Hoier, Seth Hoier, welcome to Colorado Springs," he said holding out a big hammy fist to shake hands. "Where ya be comin' in from?"

"Hello," said Roy, offering his hand in return, "I'm Roy McQuaid; this is my wife Kate and our son Shane. We're from St Louis, headed for California. We stopped in for some supplies."

"Well, we got purtnear anythin ya could possibly be ah needin in here," said Seth, "Jus have a look see and help yerself. Lemme know if ya need any help."

Roy and Kate were familiar with St. Louis general stores but nothing like Seth's. There wasn't a spare wall, support post, rafter, shelf, counter or corner that wasn't stacked, filled, piled, hanging, or otherwise occupied with merchandise.

"Much obliged," Roy answered in amazement. They picked out the basic staples - beans, potatoes, coffee, sugar, flour, bacon, salt and a 50 lb sack of oats for the horses.

Kate asked if she could buy some leaf tea, which she much preferred over the strong Arbuckle's coffee Roy drank. "Why sure ma'am, get whatever you want."

While Roy and Kate picked needed supplies, Shane had been in a trance eyeballing a myriad of jars filled with a cornucopia of assorted types and colors of candy. Roy finally noticed so he asked his wife if it was all right to let the boy get some candy. Kate looked at her enraptured son, laughed, and shaking her head said, "Sure, why not, he's earned it."

"Shane!"

"Yes sir?"

"Go ahead and get a quarter's worth of whatever you want."

"WOW! Thanks!" Shane's mouth started to water just thinking about all the choices. The thinking and choosing took a lot longer than the getting. Shane's dad finally had to hurry his son's decisions along or they would be there all day. Finally, the all-important choices were made much to the amusement of all concerned except for Shane. His choices were consequential, 'no going back, no changing of mind, final till he died', decisions!

"Guess that's all we'll need," said Roy. "What do we owe ya?"

Seth added it all up on a piece of brown paper and said, "Looks as if it'll set ya back twelve dollars and nuthin fer the candy. I ain't had so much fun watchin a kid pick candy in a long time."

That brought a laugh from everybody except Shane, who was holding his two sacks of candy as if they were bags of gold and they was all his. After Roy had paid his bill, he asked Seth what were the odds of making it thru the mountain passes before the snow totally closed them shut until spring.

"That be hard to say," Seth said scratching his beard. "It could snow four feet tomorrow, or it might not snow for another couple o' months. There's snow up in the high country but not enuff to fret about yet. Snowed two days ago up on the Peak, but she's melted by now. May still be some left on the north slope, but not more'n a couple inches."

"I understand there's only one way through these mountains and that's over Marshall Pass," said Roy.

"That be right," answered Seth. You jest follow the wagon tracks outta town to the northwest all the way through South Park till they fork at Buffler Peaks. The north route takes you to the goldfields at Fairplay. South takes you off Trout Creek Pass down to the Arkansas River. They'll be a marker there so's ya won't git' lost. My brother Ben owns a ranch 'bout a half-day's horse ride south from there. You'll have ta go right by his place. Be sure ta stop in and see 'em. They don't git many visitors out there. They'd sure appreciate the company. They wuz just in here 'bout three weeks ago."

"We'll be sure and stop," Roy said as they climbed up into the wagon, waved good-bye and headed out of town.

"What did you think of that store Son?" Kate asks. No answer. "Son!" Still no answer. Kate gave a shocked look at her husband as she turned in the wagon seat and looked thru the wagon cover into the back of the wagon. She then nudged her husband to turn and look. Turning back around, each looked at the other and broke out laughing. What caused the laugh was seeing their 12-year-old son sorting his stash of candy as if it was rare treasure. Just like a bank teller, Shane was sorting, counting and resorting his candy in various combinations. He hadn't even eaten one yet, that decision would take even longer.

"You think he might be a banker when he grows up?" Kate asked.

"I doubt it. He would never want to loan anyone any money!"

That brought another round of laughter from each.

"What's so funny?" yelled Shane.

"You are", both parents said in unison.

"Oh."

Roy and Kate just looked at each other and shook their heads. The trail took them through the foothills and over Ute Pass, west of town and to the north of Pikes Peak. They sat in silence as the wagon rolled through the most beautiful scenery they had ever seen. Shimmering quaking aspen in colors of gold and red and evergreen lined the trail. There were mule deer everywhere and similar animals that they had never seen which were much larger and a different color than deer.

"Those must be elk," Roy said. "I didn't expect 'em to be that big. Heck they're as big as a horse, and look at those antlers!"

There was a herd of about twenty grazing on the hill above them. The bull was cream colored with a dark brown head and legs, sporting a beautiful magnificent rack. As if he knew he was the object of their admiration, the bull gave a loud bugle call and shook his head for effect.

"I've never seen anything so beautiful," Kate said. Just then, Shane stuck his head out of the covered wagon.

"Wow, they're so big!" Shane added excitedly. "Bet he could whip ten of those deer we have in Missouri."

"I expect he could," his father agreed.

They traveled through this beautiful land for two more days before they reached the top of Wilkerson Pass and looked down into the Bayou Salado. The ground they had just covered fascinated and amazed them but did little to prepare them for the view that opened up before them now. They were overcome with the majesty of the spectacular mountain wonderland that spread out without end in every direction as far as they could see. Roy halted the wagon and they sat there as if in a trance.

Far off to the west, jagged, snowcapped mountains tore holes in the sky. The verdant valley floor was covered with a dazzling carpet of purple sage and wildflowers of every kind.

Dark thunderclouds in the west were coming their way so Roy wisely decided they would camp here for the night. He drove the wagon into a dense thicket of evergreen, unhooked the horses and rigged a tarp to protect them. Shane led them underneath and gave them some oats.

It would be dark in a couple of hours and this seemed to be a safe place to get out of the rain. Kate built a fire with wood Shane had gathered and made a pot of coffee. She warmed some sourdough biscuits, leftover beans and roasted two fat rabbits Roy shot the day before. They ate supper and talked about how beautiful the land was.

"I wonder if California looks like this," Shane asked.

"I don't know," Roy said, "but I can't imagine any place being as purty as this."

"I agree," Kate said, "not only is it beautiful but there is something else that I cannot put into words. It's like God went out of His way to create more beauty and wonder here than any other place."

With the setting of the sun, it rapidly turned cold. Roy and Shane cleaned the supper dishes as Kate made their beds in the wagon. They all sat around the fire listening to the thunder drawing closer and closer. Light rain began to fall with the lighting and thunder right behind it. They could feel the ground tremble with each drum roll until the sky suddenly split open over their heads. This sent them running for the relative safety of the wagon.

Inside the wagon, the rapid concussions of thunder shook not only its occupants but also the sturdy wagon itself. Lightning lit up the night sky. Cymbals of thunder crashed against earth and atmosphere like a giant celestial orchestra. Their camp, in a thick patch of evergreen, offered a surprisingly safe and dry place from the rain. The inhabitants peered out from the back of the wagon to enjoy the spectacular natural wonder playing out over their heads. They had never seen such an awesome display of unbridled energy.

Gigantic ragged claws of lightning ripped holes in the darkness, streaking from the sky to the ground. A huge dead Ponderosa Pine reached a gnarled finger into the darkness and gave the appearance of trying to catch one of these chards of light. On one occasion, it succeeded and was split down the middle, as if slashed by a galactic meat cleaver. Bursting into flames, it spewed fire and sparks for hundreds of feet into the night sky. It looked like a sixty-foot Roman candle burning on the open hillside. For nearly an hour this cosmic spectacle continued until it passed over, leaving a clear ebony sky filled with millions of brilliant glistening diamonds of twinkling light. The air had a clean fresh fragrance, purified by the rain.

Roy left the wagon to check the horses, hoping they hadn't been frightened off by the storm. He found them just as he left them, calmly standing under the tarp. He gently rubbed their foreheads, then went back to the wagon. He found Kate and Shane sound asleep.

He again walked out into the inky black night, stopped and turned his head upward gazing at the stars that only moments ago had been obscured. Never had he seen such a clear view of the heavens. He could not quite believe the unimaginable brilliance of all the shimmering lights suspended in the black sky above him. It filled him with a sense of awe and wonder at the beauty of God's creation. With hat in hand, he bowed his head.

"Lord, I thank You for protecting us from the storm and for showing us Your power and wonder. But most of all, for being with us on this journey. In Jesus name, amen." With that, he paused, looked heavenward one last time, and then replacing his hat, headed to bed.

It was now late September and they had barely reached the most treacherous part of the journey. Roy wondered if they should have spent the winter in Colorado Springs. He also wondered if Ben could put them up for the winter should snowstorms block the mountain pass. He hated to impose on anyone but the prospects of spending the winter in a snow bank did not appeal to him at all. They could also travel to Salida and spend the winter there. That might be better than to depend on someone else to feed his family through the winter. He could certainly pay for their keep but some people are funny about having other folks under foot. They would visit with Ben and see how things turned out. If they didn't hit it off, they could move on to Salida and spend the winter there. Roy removed his hat, and looked toward heaven. "Lord, I ask for Your guidance and wisdom. You know our concerns so we'll just trust that You've got it all worked out. I just thought I'd say thanks and I'm much obliged in advance." Roy was silent for a bit, then smiled, put his hat back on and went to prepare the wagon and hitch up the team.

The scenery in South Park was beauty beyond words to describe it. The sky was unlike any blue he had ever seen and when it filled with stars at night, he felt he was looking into the House of God. The aspen were in full fall regalia. The Rocky Mountains thrust their mighty stone cathedrals toward the heavens and formed an impregnable wall of granite that separated East from West. Snow had dusted these gray and purple battlements and sculpted breathtaking scenery that went on without beginning or end. Huge billowy white clouds were like giant ships under full sail on an infinite sea of blue sky. Around each bend, new vistas came into view even more spectacular than the one before. And so it went, on and on without finish until you finally had to stop, catch your breath and realize that only God could be the architect of something as awesome and wondrous as this.

Chapter 2

Ben's Ranch

Roy and his family made it to Ben's ranch near the first week in October. They arrived in a snowstorm and were glad to get to their destination. Ben and Sarah Hoier had lived on the ranch, alone, for about fifteen years. They moved from Virginia to Colorado Springs with Seth and his wife, Anna, about thirty years earlier. Ben and Seth had owned a large ranch east of the city in 'the flats' and had done well selling cattle to the cavalry and the people living in town and up and down the Front Range. When an opportunity came to purchase a huge tract of land near Salida, Ben decided he would start a cattle ranch there. Seth wanted to stay behind and run a general store. He had a bad hip that made it hard for him to stay on a horse and figured he wouldn't be able to support the ranch with that kind of a handicap.

Ben was like his brother, a little shy of six foot, barrel chested, but slimmer than Seth, with thinning gray hair, bright brown eyes and a weathered face that had multiple laugh lines. Sarah was an attractive woman even though she was approaching 60. She stood about five and a half feet tall and looked like she knew how to work. She had curly blond hair that seemed to go ever which way, but on her it looked good. She possessed a twinkle in her pale blue eyes and a ready smile. She was the perfect helpmate for Ben as she was prone to remind him. And he the same to her; they were a perfect match.

Ben and Sarah were always glad to have guests. Few people ever passed by way out here. Roy introduced himself and his family and told Ben he had met his brother in Colorado Springs. If it was possible, Ben was even friendlier than Seth, and Roy knew right away he liked this man. They unloaded what they needed for the night from the wagon as Sarah prepared a meal to celebrate their arrival.

It was a wonderful occasion when people dropped in and it was cause for a celebration. Sarah fixed venison, cornbread, mashed potatoes with gravy, and spiced apples with brown sugar.

During supper, they all became better acquainted and Roy mentioned that they were trying to get to California. Ben told Roy the snowstorm had come from the southwest and likely closed off the pass for the winter. He all but begged Roy to stay and help him work the ranch until the pass opened up in the spring.

They could have the house Sarah and he had lived in for the first fourteen years they were here. They had just finished building the new one last spring. It took nearly three years to build. A magnificent two-story structure with a covered balcony encircling the top floor that afforded a breathtaking view of the surrounding countryside. The old house was only one story but big enough for Roy and his family. Ben said he would sure appreciate the company and the help because he had too much land for one man to take care of by himself anyway.

Shane was hoping and praying that his father would agree to stay. Sarah joined in and said how much she would enjoy some female company, as it got downright isolated out here in the winter and sometimes Ben was gone for days at a time. Kate and Shane liked the idea, so Roy agreed to stay on through the winter. Shane was about as excited as a boy could get. He had never seen such beautiful country and wanted to explore every inch of it.

That winter was like a paradise for Shane. He spent most of the day with his father and Ben looking after the ranch and a few hours in the afternoon studying his schoolbooks. Kate had been a schoolteacher in Saint Louis, so she made sure he kept up with his education. He found it difficult to keep his mind on his studies because he much preferred riding around this wild country on horseback. There was always so much to see. He could ride for miles in any direction and not see another soul or any sign of civilization.

The ranch was bounded on the east by the Arkansas River, the south by Squaw Creek, the north by the Englert Ranch and the west by the top of the Continental Divide. It was a good size piece of ground by any body's standard.

The weather that winter was mild with one cold spell, below zero in late January for about a week, then it started to warm up. There was plenty of snow but it only stayed on the ground for a few days at a time. In the high country, it piled up to twenty feet deep and stayed until late summer. Spring thaw would fill the rivers and streams with melted snow and the runoff created raging torrents of water in all the canyons.

Ben asked Roy several times to stay on permanently. Sarah and Kate had grown quite close and Shane had fallen head over heels in love with the place. He was an excellent horseman and had a natural ability with a rope. He was always trying to rope anything that moved, even the chickens, much to Kate's horror and Roy's delight! He was a better shot with pistol or rifle than either Ben or Roy and had provided all the game for them during the winter. It would be a heartbreaking experience for him to have to leave now. He couldn't imagine living anywhere else.

Roy had his mind set on getting to California at first but as spring grew nearer and the land got more beautiful, he fell in love with the place also. Roy checked with God first and got definite approval. His wife and son were the two happiest people in the world when he told them he had decided to stay.

Ben and Sarah were equally as happy. They had been alone out here all these years and were really looking forward to having God fearin' folk as close neighbors. Up until now, their closest neighbor was Steve Englert about four miles to the north. Steve lived there during the warmer months with his son Taylor on about five hundred acres.

To the south, the nearest neighbors lived in Salida. There was a feed store, sawmill and a small general store owned by Ben's friend Colt Wilkins, but only a handful of people lived in town.

Chapter 3

Paradise Found

The next several years saw the ranch become very productive as Shane grew into a very capable ranch hand. He had ridden to every corner of the huge ranch and would sometimes stay gone for two weeks at a time. He was so much at home in the wilderness; it just felt natural for him to be there. He enjoyed sleeping under the stars listening to the coyotes sing, watching the elk and deer and just being a part of it all.

He especially liked the far ranging trips he took. They gave him time to have personal talks with God. These one-on-one conversations would sometimes last on and off for most of the day. During these times, Shane grew in the godly stature that would serve him well, beyond his wildest dreams. God was preparing him for a destiny that would change lives forever.

Toward the end of Shane's eighteenth year, his father asked him what were his plans concerning college. He had been expecting this question for some time, but hesitated to bring it up, just in case his father might have forgotten.

Shane knew it would be good to have a formal education, but he could hardly bear the thought of leaving. He knew he should go soon because the longer he waited, the harder it would be to go and the sooner he did go the sooner he could get back. They had all discussed at length what he should study and finally decided veterinary medicine would be a good field. There was an excellent school for this in Boston. To Shane, it seemed like it was a million miles away from home and his mountains.

One day Ben suggested, "Shane when you head to school, take one of the ranch horses, leave it with Seth to sell. When you get back, he will have a new one for you."

"Yessir, Mr. Hoier, I'll do just that."

Early on a bright clear day, in the month of June of 1873, at 19 years of age, Shane began his long journey to Boston, Massachusetts, and veterinary school.

Before Shane left, Roy prayed a short prayer, asking a blessing for his son. Shane hugged his mother and father, Ben and Sarah, and said he would see them in three or four years. He mounted up, pointed his horse east and rode out of the yard, with his mom again reminding him to write! Almost immediately, a feeling of quiet and sadness came over the ranch. It would be hard not having the youngster around with his energy and enthusiasm. They all stood in the yard with tears in their eyes until long after Shane was out of sight.

Chapter 4

Ol' Tom

Shane knew an old rancher named Tom McIntyre, who had a large spread over in South Park country north of Waugh Mountain. It was a day's ride from Ben's place and Shane thought he would spend the first night there. Tom had a cabin high up on the slope of the mountain with a breathtaking view of Black Mountain to the north. It had been almost a year since Shane had seen Tom and he was looking forward to the visit. Tom might be in his late 70's, but he was just as spry and quick as someone half his age.

Shane rode over a rise and looked down into a small meadow surrounded by aspen. There were about a dozen cattle grazing peacefully, when all of a sudden they scattered like a bomb had gone off in their midst. He was just about to ask himself what had happened when he saw the answer. A full-grown grizzly had exploded out of the brush and grabbed a yearling. With one swipe of the bear's mighty paw, the calf was killed. The rest of the herd ran off in absolute panic. The grizzly dragged his prize into the timber and began to feed.

Shane made a wide detour and rode on to Tom's cabin, which produced a copious amount of barking from Tom's three hounds. Tom was standing on the porch.

"Well, howdy stranger, step down and sit a spell."

Shane dismounted saying, "Tom, I just saw a griz take down one of your calves."

"No kiddin', where'd ya see im?"

"Oh, just over the hill a piece."

"Dang, plumb sorry I missed it." Tom laughed as he shook his head. Tom was a real character. He had cattle scattered all over a couple thousand acres and he lost one every now and again to a grizzly. It didn't seem to bother him much though. He explained it was part of the price he paid for living, "way the hell and gone up here and it's one less I gotta' feed this winter." In fact, he even said one time the only reason he raised cattle was to keep the grizzly around. He said it made his life more interesting. He did tend to get a might excited when one would show up in his front yard as one did a few years back and bit the tail off one of his hounds. Tom managed to run it off with a load of buckshot before it did any more damage. There hadn't been another one through his place since then. From time to time one might come out of the timber above the cabin and smell around but in general, they stayed out of sight. In all his years, that was the only narrow escape he had.

There were many black bears but they wouldn't come around with the dogs. Maybe Tom had a pact with the bears—he provided them with beef and they left him alone otherwise.

Shane told Tom he was headed east to attend veterinary college in Boston, Massachusetts.

Tom looked intently at Shane, "Time was when education wuzn't so important. It was and still is easy ta live off the land but tha times a comin' when a man'll need an education ta git by. We'll see it happen in my lifetime when people come by here two maybe three times a week instead of half that many in three months. I can see this land bein' divided into small pieces and sold to ranchers who'll kill the bear, wolf and coyote. Those ranches will need people the likes a' you ta doctor their horses and cows. Get all the education ya can, son, don't memorize; learn, and then learn some more. While yer at it, don't forget yer spiritual development neither. It won't do ya a dang bit o' good to get school learnin' and not God's learnin', cuz there'll come a time when book learned medicine won't fix what's wrong. You'll have ta go ta The Great Physician fer yer help."

Tom surprised Shane by the depth and insight of what he had just said. He purposed in his heart to remember the words. He also couldn't imagine this great land being overrun with people and cattle and becoming civilized. He didn't think he could live here if that were to happen.

"They'll run tha' dang railroad through here and kill all the buffler too," Tom continued. "When yer' my age, you won't be able ta sling a dead skunk without hitting somebody's dad burn fence! There's a few good years left son, but bad times is a comin'."

Shane was silent. He didn't know what to think and he didn't know what to say. He just couldn't imagine how things could change so much, so fast.

Tom broke the silence, "Wuz down on the Badger this mornin' and caught me a mess o' Cutthroat Trout. Gonna fry 'em up fer supper and yer welcome ta join me. Got too many to eat all by myself."

"I reckon I got a good long trip ahead of me. I best get some vittles in my belly. Thanks fer the invite."

The fried fish, sourdough biscuits and coffee tasted mighty good. He hadn't eaten since breakfast.

After supper, he told Tom to go sit on the porch and he would clean up. When he finished, he joined Tom. They sat in the dark listening to the sounds of the wilderness and talking about things in general. They talked about life and death, marriage and other topics of depth and importance. They discussed heaven and hell, religion, God's way verses man's, weather and the plight of the Indians. They talked until late into the night. Shane felt he got a significant portion of his education from that old man before he left.

Early next morning Tom was up cooking his sourdough biscuits with slab bacon and hen eggs. Shane was surprised to see fresh eggs since Tom didn't own any chickens.

"Where in tarnation did ya find those chicken eggs?"

Tom looked at him real serious like and said, "Well, that be tha dangest thing. The other day a bunch of um flew over tha cabin and lit right out thar in tha tall grass. I wuz gonna' shoot me a few but sumthin stopped me, so I jest let 'um alone.

Well sir, next mornin, they wuz gone but I guess they wuz thankful I didn't shoot none of um cuz they left these here fresh eggs!"

Shane had been packing his saddlebags to leave. With that, he looked straight at Tom, his mouth open wide enough to swallow his fist. "You don't mean it? Where did they come from?"

"Dang if I knowed" Tom said as serious as he could manage.

"Golly, if that ain't somethin'. I got to write dad about that."

Tom almost lost it with that one; he had to turn around quick to hide his face. After breakfast, Shane shook Ol' Tom's hand and said he'd see him in three or four years. Just before he got out of earshot, he heard Tom call. He turned his horse around and waved. That was when he heard, "Hay, Tenderfoot, chickens don't fly!" What ol' Tom didn't tell Shane was how to preserve fresh eggs for more than a month. That would have to wait until next time!

"Dang, if Tom didn't git the last word in!" Shane thought as he rode off. He promised himself to write Tom, every now and then to let him know how he was getting along.

Four days later Shane rode up to Seth's general store. Seth was sure glad to see the boy again. Shane had been to town many times in the past seven years, since they had been living with Ben, and they were all close friends.

He told Seth everyone at the ranch was doing fine. However, he was a little concerned about Ol' Tom. He related as how on his way down to town, he had stopped to visit with Tom. Shane got a worried look on his face as he related how Tom said he saw a flock of chickens fly over his cabin and roost in the tall grass. Because he didn't shoot any of 'em they had left him a bunch of eggs. "Now folks know chickens don't like to fly and especially across mountains!" Shane said. "Well, I jest thought ya might like ta know.

"Yeah, I sure prechate ya tellin' me" Seth said with concern in his voice and a worried look on his face. It was everything he could do not to break out laughing. However, the big news was Shane was on his way back East to school. Would Seth sell his horse with the understanding he would trade for another one when he returned. Seth said that would be fine.

Since the stage was due to leave in about two hours; Seth took him into the store and gave him a few things he might need on the trip. When Shane tried to pay for them, he wouldn't take the money.

"Yer part of the family and family don't pay. Consider it a goin' away present."

Shane thanked him profusely, shook his hand, hugged Anna, threw his saddlebags over his shoulder, said good-bye and walked down the street to the livery stable. There the stage would pick him up on the start of a long and tiresome trip of over two thousand miles ending in far away Boston. As Seth and Anna watched Shane walk off, Anna said, "Do you think we should have told him about preserving fresh eggs?"

"Naugh let him find out later. Tom will get a kick out of springin the news to him when he gets back."

Chapter 5

Jason Jacobi

Jason Jacobi grew up in various squalid mining camps up and down the Front Range of the Colorado Rockies. Slight of build, standing 5 feet 10 inches, he weighed in at around 140 pounds. He always looked like he needed a shave and hair cut. He was as quick to seek any moneymaking opportunity as he was with a knife, which he much preferred to fist fighting or quick draw. Ever since Jason could remember, he craved fun and excitement. He liked to see what adventure lay around the next bend or over the next hill. He had come to live for the rush that came with taking chances. It had become who he was. Then one afternoon as he sat in a local saloon nursing a tepid beer, a large bull of a man walked up to his table. He was well dress, exuding money, status and authority.

" Mind if I join you for a moment?"

"Nope, suit yer self." Jason felt a shiver run down his spine at the sound of the man's voice, compounded all the more by looking at the man's face. It wasn't so much the hard appearance as an underlying sense of evil that increased Jason's apprehension.

"My name is Mr. Smith; I'm looking for someone to do 'little favors' for me. I was told you might be interested."

"What kind of favors?"

"Oh, maybe collecting an overdue debt, running an errand, taking care of public relations problems, things like that. You would be well paid. Are you interested?"

"This is my chance to make it big," Jason thought. Therefore, apprehension aside and with no more thought than a tick on a fat dog, Jason began doing certain 'favors' for Mr. Smith. Only later, did he discover the big man he had met was Lou Blonger, one of several men belonging to a nefarious group called 'The Syndicate'. At first, they were minor jobs, such as collecting an owed debt (Jason especially liked this part of his job), running secret errands, ensuring folks stayed happy, especially the Mayor and the Sheriff. For his efforts, he was well paid, not to mention various side activities he engaged in, which was all gravy on top.

For more than three years he lived 'high on the hog', accumulating a nice nest egg for his future retirement, which he fully expected to begin sooner than later. He had come to rely on, no, believe in, "Lady Luck" always riding on his shoulder. There was just one problem with that philosophy. Lady Luck was a very fickle woman, prone to change her allegiance at the most inopportune moment.

Jason had one other problem. He began to think he was 'A Big Toad in the Pond' and let no one say different.

This over confident, self-assured, devil-may-care attitude brought with it consequences. Jason was so wrapped up in himself, that he would never see those consequences until it was too late.

Time and Lady Luck were running out on his future. He had never known real fear. That was about to change through a series of events, which had already started and would surely play out.

Chapter 6

Boston

Boston, Massachusetts was a Big learning experience for a young man from the mountain west. To Shane, it seemed that most folks were busy making money, trying to be proper and more concerned with what they thought other people thought about them than what God thought.

Shane wasn't sure what "proper" entailed and really didn't care. He was there to study, get a degree and Get Home!

He did make friends easily and was much in demand as a storyteller of tales of huge mountains, mountain men, wild animals and Indian lore, which served to make him even more homesick. He liked to 'dress up' some of his stories a bit just to see what effect it would have on others. The reaction was usually the same. Open mouths, wide eyes and the comment, "You don't mean it....really?" To which he would look real serious and without cracking a grin say, "You're right, I don't mean it", which caused everyone to burst out laughing. The one that really got students going was the 'flyin' chickens story'. There were still classmates who weren't sure if the story was true or not.

Another story Shane liked to tell was the story of "Little Tim." It seems that one day, Tim's neighbor happened to peer over his fence and saw Tim in the garden filling in a hole. Curious about what the youngster was up to, he asked, "What ya up to thar, Tim?"

"My goldfish died and I've just buried him."

"Boy, that there sure is a big hole for a goldfish, isn't it?"

Tim patted down the last heap of dirt, then said, "That's cuz he's inside your stupid cat!"

Shane was also in much demand from the fairer sex as well, something that never ceased to amaze him. Why should a ruggedly handsome, broad shouldered young man, standing six foot four, a grip like a vise, and weighing in at 225 pounds, with the most piercing deep blue eyes and captivating smile, cause such a stir in certain quarters? Shane discovered all to soon there was a lot lacking in his knowledge of females in general, something that several were more than anxious to help him with. Fortunately, for Shane, he had a strong sense of moral right and wrong. Although many tried, Shane usually politely rejected their very forward overtures, saying he needed to get back to his studies.

There was one, though, that did cause strange feelings to which he was unaccustomed. Shane had met her at a church Bible study he attended. Her name was Mary. She was twenty-one, five foot seven, slim, shapely figure, long ash blonde hair, that she usually wore up in one of the fashions of the day, brown eyes with little gold flakes, and a smile that melted Shane's lonely heart. He liked to take long walks with her along tree lined lanes and talk about his mountains, the mountain men he knew, God's Word, and his understanding thereof. Mary always listened attentively and often asked thought provoking questions. He had never met anyone like her. She seemed to understand him, his compulsion to return to Colorado Territory, and his way of life. As time passed, they became best of friends. There was nothing that they couldn't talk about, something Shane found very refreshing and pleasant.

Mary found Shane's down-to-earth wisdom, common sense, and his love of God also refreshing. She especially found his naiveté, concerning women, something that demanded her attention. She, therefore, made it her personal assignment to educate him on the subject, for his own good and especially for his protection! As time passed, she found herself becoming more and more attracted to this mountain man and was at a loss what to do about it. She knew if she continued their friendship, she would fall head-over-heels in love.

Even so, there was a nagging feeling in the back of her mind that their relationship would never work out. She knew he would never leave his mountains and live in a large city. Though she would try to push it out of her mind, it kept resurfacing. In spite of this nagging feeling, eventually she knew she was falling deeply in love with Shane McQuaid.

In their talks, Mary could not bring herself to talk about the future. She had tried once but all she got was Shane's grave concerns about the "Civilization" of the wilderness he loved and the resulting destruction thereof.

She could see and understand how much it worried him, so she would try to steer the conversation in another direction. Mary could hear her mother's words, "Trust your heart. Trust the Lord and listen to what your heart says."

"That's the problem, my mind and heart long for Shane. I have tried to resist but I am in love with this mountain man. Yet I have no peace! "Help me, Lord, to know what I should do." For some reason the heavens were silent.

One Sunday afternoon after church, as they strolled down a quite lane lined with maple trees, Mary knew it was time. It was late spring and Shane would be graduating near the end of summer, while she still had one more year of study to become a nurse. Although she fought it with every argument possible, she could not put off what she knew in her heart must be said.

Mary stopped, turned and looked up into those beautiful blue eyes and smiling face she knew so well. "Shane, you must know that I love you with all my heart and could never hurt you. I also believe what I'm about to say will not come as a total surprise. I know you have sought the Lord's wisdom concerning our future. I also sense you have been struggling with how to tell me your decision."

"Mary, please forgive me, I just can't bring myself to hurt you in any way. I care about you so very much and although we both know our futures don't seem to run along the same trail, I can't seem ta say the words."

The look of mental anguish on Shane's face tore at Mary's heart. "Then let me say them for you" she replied. With eyes that threatened to release a flood of tears, Mary said what needed to be said.

"Although I am not sure of all the reasons, we both know this relationship is not God's will for our lives. I have never met anyone for whom I have more respect and admiration. You are truly a man after God's own heart. You have given me a measuring line by which all others will be judged; for that, I deeply thank you. I realized too late, that I was falling in love with you, but I don't regret one moment of the times we have shared together. The long walks, the discussions, your sense of humor, and just being in your presence. I will cherish them always. God bless you, Shane McQuaid," she then kissed him, turned and walked out of his life.

Shane watched her walk away, paralyzed by the pain he felt in his heart. He had no words; he knew she was right, for God had not blessed this relationship. He adored her, but he knew in his heart that they could never be.

She stopped, turned around and looked straight at him. "Shane, I really do understand and eventually you will also. Yes, it's hard and yes, it hurts! However, we both love God more than self. What we want is not as important as what God wants for our lives; for our destinies. Please, my love, turn around, walk away and don't look back." With that, she turned and ran to her dorm room, fell across her bed and cried until she could cry no more. As she lay on her pillow, wet with her tears, Mary cried out to her Heavenly Father, "Lord, I love Shane so much, but I feel, in Your infinite wisdom, You have another plan for my life but right now my heart is broken. I desperately need more of Your grace and comfort. Please, Lord, take the pain away, in Jesus' name I pray."

Mary thought there were no tears left, she was wrong. Just when she thought, she would despair of life itself... "My daughter, I have chosen another for you who will fulfill your heart and desires beyond your wildest dreams, as will you for him. Be strong, hold your head up, for I will heal the hurt and give you joy unspeakable. This is your Heavenly Father who loves you and I am well pleased."

As Mary lay on her bed, her eyes puffy and red from crying, a peace came over her. It felt like liquid love was being poured from the top of her head to the soles of her feet. This time the tears she cried were ones of joy, thanksgiving and praise to the Creator of the Universe Who had heard her prayer and answered in an unbelievable way. She knew within her heart that tomorrow would be the first day of the destiny that God had set for her life and whether he knew it or not, also Shane's. God was so good!

As Shane walked back to his dorm, he felt empty inside. His heart was broken as well. He had no words or understanding of this. He was confused and hurt. Why had she walked away? Why was she telling him "she understood?" She didn't understand squat! Women! He'd never understand 'em. Dang it, they were just too plumb complicated and unpredictable! Now, you take a horse, they were loyal and dependable, well . . . some were...!

Later, as he aimlessly stood looking out his dorm window, he heard that small voice he was so use to, only this time it wasn't so small or soft!

"My son, why are you allowing Satan to control your thoughts and actions? Are you not stronger than he who is a liar with no truth found in him? The one who comes only to kill, steal, and destroy. Have you not sought Me and asked for wisdom? Did I not, without hesitation, grant that? And now, you fall back in self-pity, pride and selfishness, wanting what you know in your heart is not yours!"

It was as if someone had hit him square between the eyes with a fence post! He fell to his knees and began to cry out to his Heavenly Father.

"My Father, My Father, I humbly ask Your forgiveness, please forgive me for falling to the accuser and my own fleshly nature. Thank You for rebuking me, for I know You love me and I submit to Your will for my life. Please allow the Holy Spirit to continue to guide and direct the course of my life, for my heart's desire is to follow You. In Jesus' name I ask it, Amen."

From that day, Shane never again got sidetracked into following his flesh rather than God's will for his life.

During his medical studies and animal anatomy classes, Shane discovered that he had an ability to remember everything, even the most minute details of his subject matter. He graduated with high marks and praise from the Dean of Veterinary Science.

The very formal graduation ceremony was agony for Shane. He turned to a friend and asked, "Man, when will this shindig be over?" The friend, seeing a golden opportunity for payback said, "Oh,... in about two more hours!" Those seated nearby suddenly heard an audible groan.

When the commencement program was finally over, albeit much shorter than his friend had initially led him to believe, Shane packed his few possessions and said his goodbyes.

He looked for Mary but she was nowhere to be found. The next day he caught the first of several trains that would eventually lead to St. Louis, that would then connect to the new Kansas and Pacific into Denver. He was headed home at last, HALLELUJAH! If he could have sprouted wings and flown, he would have done it!

Chapter 7

I got it!

As Shane had weeks and over two thousand miles worth of travel to reluctantly look forward to, he spent a lot of time either daydreaming, sleeping, reading his well-worn Bible, or studying two books he had bought while at school - The American Cattle Doctor and The Modern Horse Doctor. One of his older professors had recommended them and said that, if he could find them, they would be invaluable to his further education. He also added, "You'll also learn more sticking your hand up a cow's rear end than any college book!" Laughing, Shane said he would definitely remember that!

Shane stared out the smoke grayed train window. He was now twenty-two; it had been over three long years since he had seen this view.

His studies should have taken four years but he was a driven man. He didn't take summers off, attending classes year round. He felt he was called to be a veterinarian but there was a deeper longing, so deep that nothing could stand in his way. The initial cultural shock of attending school in a large city like Boston, was almost overwhelming, not to mention trying to adapt to a life style completely foreign to what his life had become in Colorado Territory. He praised God for the excellent tutoring he got from his mom.

And now he was traveling by train over the same trails that had been traversed only by horseback and stagecoach. More than anything, Shane wanted to be back home, deep in his beloved mountains. The Rockies, a place where he could breath, where he didn't feel hemmed in, a place where he could spend uninterrupted time with God, and revel in all His wondrous creation. Home, where his folks, his friends and the critters, called "home".

To help kill the time, Shane liked to read Proverbs because it contained more condensed wisdom than anywhere else in the Bible. He also loved Psalms for the prose, poetry and songs of praise. For every emotion or mood, he could find a psalm to match. Shane tended toward the praise psalms, but he also discovered the reality of the equally persistent enemies who sneer, hurt and plot violence that appear in nearly every psalm. He understood that faith in God was a struggle against powerful forces that often seemed more real than God. He had discovered that the writers of Psalms frequently felt abandoned, misused and betrayed, much as he initially had at school.

He prayed reverently that he would never question his faith or lose his trust for his Heavenly Father. He knew from personal experience that God was real and that the Bible was the road map for ones journey through life. He prayed he would never lose the map until he had it committed to heart, at least the important parts!

This particular day, as the train chugged its way west, through flat Kansas, Shane again began re-reading the Book of Acts.

He liked the Book of Acts because it read like well-written history. It followed a logical plan, included fascinating details and dramatic events. It made sense to a young man brought up to seek the truth and know the truth when he found it. That's why, when he got to the second chapter of Acts, suddenly the words started popping off the page. He'd read these same verses before. Therefore, why all of a sudden did they seem to be highlighted? As he read on, a stirring began deep in his heart, even down into his very soul. All of a sudden, a prayer began tumbling out of his mouth. "Lord, I want what they got! I want tha whole barrel ah goods! Fill me with your Holy Spirit like you did those men in Acts! The whole of it, Lord, ... if ya please!"

All of a sudden, like a coffee pot starting to bubble on a campfire, a beautiful new language started pouring forth from Shane's lips. "What in the world is this," he thought, "Holy Cow! I Got It! I Got It!" Shane shouted. "Whoopee!" THAT, was when he realized he was standing up in a swaying rail coach, with everybody looking at him like a calf looks at a new gate, or a top cowhand looking at an empty lasso loop he just threw at a slow moving cow and missed! Shane promptly sat down, pulled his hat lower on his forehead and commenced to reading, silently! Boy, his insides sure weren't quiet. He thought he would bust! He wanted to get up and do a jig but thought better of it since the conductor was staring a hole through him just then!

Chapter 8

Retirement Plan

On a summer day in late June 1876, Lew Blonger summoned Jason to his office on the bottom floor of the Elite Saloon on Stout Street and asked him to hide and care for a special black horse. The job would include a pay increase if Jason did as he was instructed, with no problems, that is.

Jason jumped at the chance as fast as a striking snake. He was cautioned, that no one must know about the horse and if anything happened; Jason would be held accountable. Jason wasn't worried; he hadn't had any trouble in the past that he couldn't fix. So, why should he worry now?

Besides, 'Lady Luck' was still riding on his shoulder. Once a week Jason was to report to Blonger concerning this special horse. Blonger again reminding him that he would be held accountable if anything happened to the horse.

During the last year, however, Jason had become dissatisfied with working for Blonger. "I'm destined for bigger and better things. I'm tired of being treated like a lackey, used only to run errands, and do all the dirty work," he thought.

This was when Jason got a brilliant idea. Why not steal the horse, sell it, and light out for parts unknown? Jason thought of himself as a rather crafty fellow. He assumed it would be "as easy as lickin' butter off a knife." The first thing to work out was "when". The timing had to be just right.

Two months later around ten o'clock at night, Jason was holding sway at his favorite saloon, The Ginn Mill, a rowdy establishment, located on Larimer Street in Denver. It was one of the more disreputable watering holes, serving draft beer, Rock-gut Rye and Who-Hit-John Whiskey, at a nickel a shot. It had a bordello on the second floor if you got tired of the happenings on the main floor.

Suddenly, a seedy looking character entered the saloon and approached him as he sat drinking a mug of beer at a table with some of his fair weather friends. The stranger, known only as Sweeney, was medium height, strongly built, roughly clothed, beefy fists with several scars showing and a lined face that came from hard living. He had an ugly knife scar that ran across the bridge of his nose and part of his right cheek. He tried, without much success, to conceal the scar with a scraggly beard. His eyes continually darted about. He looked meaner than a one-eyed rattler with an attitude. He carried a hide-away pistol in a shoulder holster, concealed by a short-wasted coat and a Tennessee Toothpick in his right boot. He wore a well-worn English Bowler hat that was pulled forward and cocked to the right. . In general, a very unpleasant looking fellow, indeed.

With a sardonic grin and a raspy voice he said, "You be Jacobi"?

"That's right, whadaya want"? Jason responded, angry that he had been disturbed.

"I needs ta have a chats wit ya about a private matter."

"Beat it, I'm busy"!

"Ye best hear what's I gotta say, iffin' you know what's good fer ya."

"Who sent ya"?

"Yer boss".

"Alright, I'll meet ya in the back room as soon as I finish my beer," Jason growled. He didn't like the setup, but he had a feeling he had best see what Sweeney wanted since he also did work not only for Blonger but also for Soapy Smith, another noted crime boss in Denver.

"Well, don't takes long, I ain't got all night." With that, the stranger turned and shuffled off toward the back of the saloon.

"Well, guess I'd better go see what the critter wants," which brought a laugh from those around the table. He downed the last of his tepid beer and rose from the table. "I'll be back, keep my seat warm, preferable with tha blond over there." This brought another laugh.

As Jason entered the small windowless room, he noticed the stranger leaning up against a back corner smoking a short stub of a rank smelling stogie.

"Ok, I'm here, whadaya want?"

"It ain't what I wants, it's what Mr. Blonger wants and he's gittin' might antsy. He wants ta know why he ain't heard from ya." The stranger took a drag off his stogie and blew a cloud of thick smoke slowly at Jason.

Jason knew he had to think quickly! "Tell Blonger there's no problem. I got a tip that a gang was out to steal his horse, so I had to move him to a different location outta town. I just ain't gotten around ta lettin' tha boss man know yet. Everything is back on track, not to worry."

Jason could feel sweat running down his side, "Don't look nervous, stay calm, and everything'll work out," he kept telling himself.

Sweeney eyed him closely. It seemed he could see right through him. Jason's heart started to race and he began to sweat more. "So ya say . . . we'll see."

As quick as a snake, he had Jason by the throat, pushed up against the wall. "Tomorrow, without fail, deliver tha horse, you know the place...ya hears?"

Gasping, Jason nodded his head. With that, the stranger released his grip, brushed past him, disappearing out of the saloon into the dark night, trailing a thin cloud of smoke.

"Well, smart is as smart does and I ain't no dummy," Jason thought, as he tried to regain his composure. "My financial plan has worked just fine so far. I'll soon be in high cotton for life." With that thought pleasantly running around in his ego-inflated mind, he said good-bye to his companions and took a circuitous route back to his place to pack. As he neared completion, he stopped and removed a loose floorboard from inside his small clothes closet. Reaching in, he lifted out a large stack of bills and a small leather pouch of gold nuggets that he had liberated from a very drunk miner. Placing these in the bottom of the other saddlebag, he then proceeded to fill the remaining space with cooking gear and other supplies. Satisfied he had forgotten nothing; he undressed, got into bed and fell into a fitful sleep. At sunup the next morning, he closed, locked his door, and walked a back way to the livery stable, saddled his horse, told the stable boy he would be back in four days and quietly left town by a back road. He headed northwest toward the mountains. A few miles outside of town, just around a bend in the trail, he turned off and rode into a clump of nearby cedar trees, pulled up and waited, silently watching his back trail. After about thirty minutes, certain he was not followed, he headed southwest, skirting town heading for Colorado Springs. As he crossed the South Platte River the following afternoon, he swung west for about a mile, as a crow flies, where, at an abandoned miner's shack, he picked up the black mare, then proceeded due South at a steady gallop toward Colorado Springs. He figgered it was a smart move. No one knew him there and no one would ask questions.

By late morning three days after leaving Denver, Jason had completed his business, not to his liking, but with the Pike's Pike Gold Rush and an influx of westward bound travelers, he had to take whatever he could find. He wasted no time heading south toward Santa Fe and then El Paso. As the sun began to slide behind the Rocky Mountains to the West, Jason was already miles south of Colorado Springs.

Even though things were going according to schedule, he could not shake the feeling someone was watching him, though he saw no one. "Ah, just my imagination from being tired and all," he thought. Later as the last light of day began to fade, Jason pulled off the dusty road to the west where he had seen a stand of cottonwoods in a shallow draw and began to make camp for the night.

BANG! A shot rang out, piercing the dusk like a streak of lighting. At first, the only thing Jason felt was the blood that began running down the right side of his face. As he reached up to touch his cheek, the searing pain, like a hot poker, hit him full force.

Numbing fear returned with a vengeance. "They've found me; I've got to get out of here"! That was Jason's last thought as he reached for his pistol and everything went black.

With the return of consciousness, so did the searing pain. Reluctantly, Jason opened his eyes. Looking up, he saw an ugly face partly illuminated by the fire. "Wish I'd have kept my eyes closed!" He thought.

He didn't need to ask whom the face belonged to, he knew. He also knew he was a dead man if he could not distract Scar Face, aka Sweeney, long enough to be able to pull his knife from his right boot.

"Where ya be headin' Jacobi?"

"Are you crazy, why did ya shoot me?"

"I'll only ask ya one more time, where ya be headin' and where's our property!"

The glint, caused by the fire, in Scar's eyes sent shivers down Jason's spine.

"Listen you idiot, I had ta make a run with some supplies to tha minin' camp down at Cross Creek. Then I was plannin' ta head back ta town and get the horse. I told the kid at tha livery stable when I'd be back.

Sweeney turned toward the fire to pick up something. As he did, Jason reached for his boot knife, but he was a might slow and it cost him his life with a bullet right between the eyes. Sweeney looked down at the dead man and cussed. "Died before he could talk, Blonger ain't gonna like this."

That same night, at 1628 Stout Street, in a private upstairs room of the Elite Saloon owned by Blonger, a group of six men were seated around an oval table. At first glance, they gave the appearance of a group of businessmen conducting a board meeting. This was far from the truth, for although they were indeed businessmen, of a sort, their association with any legal business venture was misleading. They cared less about others than a flea on a fat dog! Some smoked custom rolled cigars, made to their specifications, shipped from the East Coast. All drank vintage brandy from hand blown crystal goblets. Each man seemed at ease and self-assured with himself. Why shouldn't they be? Each had his hand in at least one or more kinds of con, graft, gambling saloon, prostitution, smuggling or grubstake scam. For years, these and others like them had engaged in deadly turf wars for bigger and bigger pieces of the money pie. That was, until Lew Blonger stepped in and through various means formed a loose knit organization known as 'The Syndicate'. The Syndicate had a very select set of rules that, if broken, had only one penalty, death. The benefits had outweighed the restrictions so its members had agreed to follow the rules for their mutual benefit, so far.

"Gentleman, we may have a problem, said Blonger. It was his face, not his size, that struck people with an instant uneasy feeling, as if he were 'on the prod' and someone to avoid, if possible. "It appears our friend Mr. Jacobi may have decided to double cross us in the matter of the black horse." At that, a chorus of angry voices rose as one. Most, reminding Blonger how much money they had invested in the racehorse.

"Gentlemen, calm down! I have instructed my associate to deal with this matter and locate our property at all costs. He feels certain, barring any unseen difficulties, to be able to glean what information Mr. Jacobi has, one way or the other. I will let you know the outcome at our next meeting, a week from today. In the meantime, let us discuss ways to further solidify our control of, shall we say. . .other forms of business that have proven very lucrative for our organization."

Chapter 9

Lady

A fter what seemed an eternity, Shane finally reached Denver. After a restless night in a local hotel, early the next morning, he took the Overland Stage to Colorado Springs. Compared to Denver, the Springs was still a small, quite community nestled at the base of the eastern slope of the Rockies. Overlooking, like a giant sentinel, was snow-capped Pikes' Peak, towering to 14,110 feet and serving as a landmark for westward bound travelers that would have to traverse Marshall Pass to the west. He was shocked at how fast Denver, once a small dirty mining town, had now become a busy settlement full of buildings and people. Ol' Tom's predictions were coming true, much to Shane's disappointment.

When the stage finally stopped in Colorado Springs, Shane jumped from the coach, caught his saddlebags that were tossed down to him, looked up at Pikes Peak, filled his lungs with pure Colorado air and felt like letting out a loud yell, but thought better of it. He didn't want to waste any more time here than necessary, trying to convince the sheriff that he wasn't crazy or drunk, just glad to be back home. He walked up the street to Seth's general store, walked in, and seeing no one, bellowed out, "What's a fella gotta do to get some service around here?"

All of a sudden he heard a squeal, "Shane! Seth, its Shane! He's come back," Anna shouted, as she rose from behind a counter to see who was making such a ruckus. She ran over, reaching up to hug him as Seth came out of the back room and hurried over to shake his hand and give him a bear hug.

"It's good to see you agin, young fella and welcome back. Yer folks wuz just in here a couple weeks ago. They didn't know when you'd be through for sure, but thought it would be within the month. They sure have missed ya boy. They're all doin' fine, got cattle running all over tarnation up there. Shor, need someone to help em with tha ranch."

Seth and Anna invited Shane in for a bite to eat because he looked mighty hungry. Why wouldn't he be, considering his size? While Anna was serving him, he asked Seth about a horse. "Funniest thing bout that. Thar wuz a fella in here a few days ago lookin ta trade fer a wagon. Ya got ta see this animal!" After lunch, Seth and Shane went out to see this wonder horse. "She sure is a fine lookin animal," Shane said. " Must be eighteen hands."

"Eighteen and a half," said Seth.

"Well, lemme see," Seth scratched his beard and said," The difference 'tween what I sold yer horse fer and what I got in this here mare means I owe ya $20." He threw Shane a $20 gold piece. "She's all yers boy, don't know that thar's another one like her in the whole country."

Shane could hardly believe it. He never expected to be able to have a horse like this. They went for thousands of dollars back East. That was more money than he could make in his whole life. He knew horses and this was one of a kind. The mare was truly a magnificent animal, her coat shown like a piece of hard black coal. Her mane and tail full and shiny. She had a perfect shaped star blaze on her forehead and big beautiful bright eyes. When she moved, she was grace in motion, her muscles rippling in all the right places. Her overall confirmation was perfect; Shane was in love with this horse!

"How'd ya manage ta trade for this horse? Ya musta held a shotgun on the guy!"

"Weren't my business to inquire as to why he wuz so desperate to trade. He rode up trailin this horse and asked iffin I had a wagon fer sale. Said he had looked all over town and couldn't find none due to folks rushin off ta tha gold fields. He needed a wagon and another horse real bad for some reason, he wouldn't say why and all he had to sell or trade were this here horse. I had an old freight wagon and a plug of a horse I'd been tryin' to git rid of. I told him I'd trade the wagon fer tha black. He didn't like the deal much but said if I'd throw in tha horse and a few supplies; it was a deal. He gave me a bill o' sale. Bought some supplies, hooked up and lit outta town as if he had a bee in his bonnet! That's the end o' that story. Oh, did I mention to ya that horse has a mean streak? She's bit me twice." He rolled up his shirtsleeve and showed Shane where a piece of skin was missing from his forearm.

"Yer sure gittin slow in yer old age," Shane kidded. "Where's the other spot he got ya?"

Laughing, Seth said, "Well, you never mind bout that one!"

"Well my friend, I don't understand the wheres and whatfors 'bout tha' trade but I sure thank the good Lord for it and for yer tradin' ability. That being said, I'm yearnin' to get back to the high country, guess I better quit flappin' my gums, get a few supplies and head out."

After trying to pay for what he needed, Seth would not take his money. He saddled the mare with his old saddle that Seth had kept for him, tied on his saddlebags, bedroll, slicker and rifle scabbard. The entire time, the mare watched him intently, but made no threatening gestures. Anna came out to give him some fresh baked bread and a slice of ham. He gave her a big hug, shook Seth's hand, patted the mares' muscular neck and with an 'eye to eye' look, stepped into the stirrup and swung up into his saddle.

Well, I'll be, the mare didn't even flinch. Did ya see that Anna? It's as if she knowed Shane wuz supposed to be astride her! Ain't that sumthin!

"Seth, it's "The Look" I gave her. Works every time. I'll teach it to you some time.

I am much obliged to you for taking care of my gear and your Christian hospitality. Would hope that other folks were like you two. Hope to see you both again soon. Thanks so much for the great food and all that you have done. May our Lord bless you many times over for your generosity." With that, he touched the heel of his right boot to the mare's side and rode off down the dusty street giving a wave as he did.

Chapter 10

Like the Wind

Shane sensed the mare wanted to run but held her back while they were still in town, for fear she would scare some old woman to death or run over somebody. It felt like he was sitting on a keg of dynamite! As soon as he hit the foothills he let her go and she took off like a shot. Up the slow winding trail she went, at a full gallop.

"I'll bet she could outrun that train I was on," he thought to himself. On and on she ran, never letting up, never slowing down. Shane didn't have to urge her to run, she ran all by herself as if she couldn't get enough. He'd never heard of a horse like this. She ran like the wind. Heck, she could outrun the wind! He was amazed at her stamina. Down one hill and up the other side, didn't seem to matter uphill or down she just kept going. Shane lost track of time sitting in the saddle of this amazing animal.

Before he knew it, they were on top of Wilkerson Pass, looking into South Park. He was shocked! They had traveled more than forty miles in a little over an hour! The great horse was hardly breathing and wanted to run some more.

She hadn't even worked up a sweat. He felt her neck and it was cool and dry. He was just dumbfounded! No animal on God's green earth could do what they just did! Shane was getting tired and his muscles ached. He hadn't ridden much in the past three years and it would take some time to get back into shape. Once he did, what a pair they would make! He got down, tied the mare to a branch and tried to stretch the kinks out of his arms and legs. "Good Lord, what a ride," he said aloud. "You're quite a horse! Lord, you got sumthin to do with this?" All he thought he heard was a soft chuckle and a feeling of inner peace and calm. "Thank you, Lord, I'll do my best to honor your gift and give you the glory."

It took about thirty minutes before Shane was ready to ride again. He made a sandwich with the bread and ham, washing it down with water from his canteen. He then cupped his hand next to the horse's muzzle and poured water for her. Once he was back in the saddle, the mare took off like a shot once more. Down the pass and across the sagebrush flats they went, leaving a cloud of dust behind. They scared up a jackrabbit; it ran along beside them until the horse kicked it into high gear and ran off and left the jackrabbit like it was standing still. Shane was even more amazed than he was before. The mare still had more speed! She was almost faster than Shane wanted to go. If he ever fell off, he would starve to death before he stopped rolling!

He knew immediately that he was in the possession of some wonderful gift from God. A wild tornado - and he was sitting astride it! Across the sagebrush they went, Shane hanging on for all he was worth. They got to the Middle Fork of the South Platte and the mare jumped clean across to the other side and kept going never breaking stride. He would not have been surprised at this moment if the horse began to fly. He was beyond amazement now and just didn't know what to think. This horse must have been one of the horses that pulled God's 'Chariots-of-Fire" across the heavens!

The sun was going down by now, the light fading. The mare was still going strong. Shane began to feel uncomfortable, because he couldn't see where they were going. He slowed her to a trot and after a while came to a halt near a stand of aspen and a small creek.

He needed a rest; it was time to make camp. The mare didn't seem to be tired at all.

She stood patiently while Shane took off her bridal, saddle and blanket. He started to put a hobble on, but the mare seemed to become irritated or was it the hurt look she gave him? Shane wasn't sure what to do. As he was weighing his options, the mare placed her head on his broad right shoulder.

"Well I'll be, are you trying to tell me sumthin?"

The mare raised her head, looked at Shane and nodded. Shane was dumb struck.

"OK, you win, no hobble." The mare nickered and nodded her head again.

"No one would believe this even if I swore on a stack of Bibles. They would laugh me right out of the country!"

A can of hash, a can of peaches, bread from Seth's store and some coffee was supper - a simple but eloquent feast for anyone dining in the Wilderness Cafe. When he finished, he tossed the cans in the fire to burn off any leftover food. His bedroll felt good as he laid his head on the saddle and gazed up into the star filled heavens. He never failed to be awed by the vastness of the sky at night. He cared not to fully understand that all he saw was only a small part of what was there. He knew God had it all worked out; his job was just to have faith and trust in His direction.

The coals from his fire glowed red and the orange flames cast eerie shadows into the dark. Strange figures danced on the bark of the quakies.

The mare grazed quietly nearby. He fell asleep listening to the coyotes sing and dreamed he was riding his magical horse through the night sky.

Shane awoke before sun-up, built up the fire, and put last night's coffee on. He walked over to his horse, rubbed her neck and scratched her ears while talking softly to her, which she seemed to like.

Back at the fire the coffee was boiling. He poured a cup, that by now was strong enough to hold a spoon up and chewed on a piece of beef jerky. This would have to suffice for breakfast. He doused the fire with the rest of the contents of the coffee pot. He fetched several more from the creek to make sure it was completely out. He then crushed the two cans from supper and buried them so the sharp metal would injure no animal.

After breaking camp and saddling the mare, he led her to the creek for a drink. He looked around at this wild country and took a deep breath; he was glad to be back. After the mare had her fill of water, Shane climbed into the saddle and headed west. He held her back for a few minutes to get the feel of the saddle again. Once he had the rhythm, he let her go. She took off like the day before and he hung on for dear life. He had never known speed like this. It was incredible, it was beyond words.

The train seemed infinitely slow compared to his horse. The ground passed by underneath at a heart stopping speed and the cool wind in his face made his eyes water. It was exhilarating to see the countryside pass by so fast.

Everything went by in a blur. Mile after mile they went like this at full gallop. Shane was afraid she would go even faster if he touched her flank with the reins. He dared not do that, this was fast enough for now, at least until he got back into shape.

At last he came to a small rise that overlooked Ol' Tom's cabin where he halted to survey the area. He learned never to approach any cabin without checking out the lay of the land. He could see the old rancher sitting on the porch so he rode down to chat a spell.

"Well, will ya lookie what the cat drug in? Mighty kind of ya ta drop by and visit an ol' man. Yer tha first person I seen in weeks!"

When he left Tom the last time, because of what he had said, Shane was expecting to see new houses all over the place when he got back. He was glad that civilization hadn't smothered this part of the mountain yet.

"It's good to see ya again, Tom," he said as he dismounted. He took the mare over to the water trough and loosened her girth cinch.

"Where'd ya git' that fine looking horse? Ain't never seen one like that."

"I gave my old horse to Seth when I left for school. When I returned, he gave me this horse and $20 to boot just to take her off his hands. He said she had a mean streak, even took a couple o' bites outta him." Shane laughed and said, "He showed me the one on his arm, but wouldn't show the other. I got a good idea where it was though."

Tom laughed, "Yer probly right, I'll have ta remember ta ask him bout that 'other place' next time I'm over his way. Son, ya shor gotta' dang good bargain. Iffin' I need a new horse, I'll let ya do the dealin'!"

"Well, to be honest, that ain't no ordinary horse. I firmly believe she is a gift from God. She can run faster than any horse you'll ever see." He sat down on the steps while Tom went inside to get him a cup of coffee.

Shane asked Tom how things had been.

"Same as always. The grizzlies is still here. I saw my first wolf last winter! Just woke up one mornin' and there he was, standin' on the edge o' tha timber above the house. Watched him fer a good long while afore he disappeared. First one I seen in all these years."

They talked about the school Shane graduated from and about the country back there.

They talked about the plains and how people lived out there in the middle of nowhere in a hole in the ground surrounded by sod bricks, burnin Buffalo chips for fuel and about trains and how glad Shane was to be back.

"Yer folks is fine but they sure been missin' ya. They wuz here a time er two and I rode over ta visit 'em a couple times. Yer the only thing they talked about the whole time. Ya better git on back there so they can have some peace and quiet.

"Yeah, yer right, I'm really looking forward ta gittin' home. I'll stop in from time to time and see what mischief ya been up to. The Lord be with ya and see ya safe, my friend."

"You also son, God Bless ya."

Chapter 11

Reunion

At the ranch, Sarah and Kate had the houses all ready for Shane when he showed up. Shane had sent a letter to Seth telling him to send it to his folks with the first rider headed past Ben's ranch.

In the letter which had arrived a month ago, Shane said he would be headed home the end of August. They didn't know exactly when he would arrive but they had cooked, canned and put welcome signs up all over the place. They could hardly wait for him to arrive. It might not be until next month but they would be ready. Roy and Ben were up on the roof of the old house fixing a hole when they saw a lone rider off in the distance.

"Rider comin", Ben hollered down to the women.   Both ladies ran out on the porch, but he was too far away to see who it was. They were afraid to let themselves believe it might be Shane in case it was just another rider. They had been waiting for him for so long, it just didn't seem possible that it could finally be him. They were expecting to find out it was just someone passing through, but just in case, they would watch a little while longer. The rider went down into a ravine and disappeared. They waited a few minutes and then a few minutes more and finally they were about to give up when the rider came into sight again.

"IT'S SHANE!" Roy yelled from the top of the house. "IT'S SHANE, IT'S REALLY SHANE!" he choked, his voice breaking as his eyes filled with tears.

They nearly fell trying to get down from the roof. The women were just beside themselves with anticipation. They were hugging each other and then hugging the men and jumping and screaming as Shane rode into the yard and dismounted into a mob of hugs, kisses, hand shaking, backslapping and tears. They were all so overcome with emotion they couldn't talk. They all just held on to one another tightly, half-afraid that this might just be a dream and they would wake up and Shane wouldn't be there like all the dreams before. However, this one seemed to hold because when they opened their eyes, Shane was still there and they realized their boy was back. Their long wait was over.

Ben was the first one able to speak. "I never thought I'd be so glad to see someone in my life. You are the only thing these women have talked about in months. It's good to have ya back."

Roy choked back some more tears and said, "Let me say a prayer." They all held hands and bowed their heads and Roy said a simple but eloquent prayer thanking the Lord for the safe return of their boy. Neither Kate nor Sarah trusted themselves to speak. Neither had control of their emotions, they just held on to him, afraid to let go.

"You all go into the house and I'll tend to the horse." Ben said. Kate put her arm around her son and they went inside.

"I've been ridin' hard to get here and I'm plumb tuckered out," Shane said. "I had my hands full with that mare. Fastest horse I ever saw, it was all I could do to hang on. Woulda taken me two more days to get here on any other animal. Seth gave me $20 to take that mare before he hurt himself tryin' to ride her. He said she was kinda mean, but I didn't have any trouble."

"Maybe I should go help put her up for the night." Roy and Shane walked to the barn where Ben was brushing Lady, who was as calm as you please.

"She's a beauty," Roy said. Seth must need spectacles or they taught ya a thing or two about horse tradin' at that fancy school back East!"

"I was just tellin' Mom that Seth gave me $20 to take her. Told me he just couldn't handle a horse like that."

Ben finished brushing the mare, gave her some oats, and they returned to the house.

Sarah and Kate began to set the table for the feast they had planned for weeks. They had baked fresh bread that morning, several pies, cookies and a carrot cake from carrots they picked from the garden. There was a ham, apple preserves, corn on the cob, cider, venison and more. Seemed like enough food to feed fifty people.

It was a happy time for everybody and a celebration was in order that they would never forget. Before they began to eat, Roy said another prayer, a longer one with much emotion, thanking the Lord once again for the safe return of their son. His words were so eloquent; they were all in tears.

After supper, the women set about cleaning up the kitchen and the men went outside to sit on the porch. They talked about the last three years, what the East was like, what the school was like, and how the people were. They talked and talked and when the women joined them, Shane had to repeat everything he just said; then they talked some more. They had so much to talk about and catch up on. They talked late into the night until Shane couldn't keep his eyes open any longer, so they all headed to bed. Roy said another short prayer and Shane was asleep before his head hit the pillow.

Everyone slept in a little later than usual the next morning. Shane slept until awakened by the smell of fresh coffee and sourdough biscuits cooking. When he finally realized he was home, he threw back the covers, jumped out of bed or rather he started to jump out of bed, until his sore muscles said, 'Wait a minute Bub! Not so fast! Shane had to do some stretching before he could get dressed. Then he 'walked' into the kitchen, hungry as a bear.

His mom and dad were sitting at the table. "Good mornin'," they both said. His mother got up and gave him a big hug. "I've missed you so much. I could hardly stand it these past three years. I got to thinking you might never come back."

"I've missed both of you just as much. Many times I was ready to give up and come home. However, I knew I couldn't live with myself for being a quitter, so I got buried in my studies and tried not to think about it. On the day of graduation, I thought they would never quit talking. I've seen enough of civilization and don't care if I never see it again!"

"Well, I felt, in reading your letters, you were struggling and didn't care for the country back east. Could you be more specific about what didn't sit well with ya," Roy asked.

"Dad, it seemed that most of those folks were in such a busy hurry that they really didn't have time for living. God created many wonderful things for us to enjoy, and not just take for granted. I did get involved in a Bible study at a local church near the college that I very much enjoyed. I learned a lot but there just seemed to be something missing. I didn't know what it was back then, but I shore do now!"

"And what might that be Son?"

"Well, I'm not sure what the proper terminology is, but it's what happened in the Book of Acts. It happened to me!"

"Could you be a little more specific about this 'happening' thing?"

"Well, first off, I was readin the book of Acts. Now, I've read that book several times, but it was different this time. I got this funny feelin deep down in my spirit that something was goin' ta happen. All I needed ta do was ask in faith and believe. So, I did jest that. I asked! Then, all of a sudden, strange words that I don't understand started pouring out of me, my mouth that is. I can't really explain it, except it is the most wonderful feelin I've ever had. It even tops when you let me buy all that candy at Hoier's General Store or the first time I kissed a purty girl! If you can explain it any better, I would sure appreciate it."

Roy and Kate were about to bust with joy and excitement. As calmly as Roy could he said, "Shane, what you experienced was an 'Infilling of the Holy Spirit. Some call it Baptism in the Holy Spirit. What you call it is not as important as the fact that what you have received is a greater dose of God's Spirit, His heart, His very life. You got the Holy Spirit when you got saved. But, there's more, so much more. Jesus Himself said He would send another who would fill you with power. I know you're on the right track Son, just keep puttin' God's Word in ya and keep askin. You will discover the richness of God's Heart and His limitless love for mankind."

"Yes Sir, I'll do just that."

Chapter 12

Back in the High Country

The next few weeks went by fast. Shane got back into the rhythm of the ranch. He was a big help taking care of the animals, immediately applying his knowledge of veterinary medicine.

He spent many hours on horseback forming an unbreakable bond with the mare. They were virtually inseparable. It seemed the more she ran, the more she wanted to run. She thrived on the pure mountain air and there was just no limit to her endurance.

Shane couldn't think of a name for her that would be adequate or appropriate enough to define her characteristics. When he spoke of her, he referred to her as "the mare" and when he spoke to her, he called her "Lady." "Ya know, I think you are a lady so, if it's OK with you, I'm gonna call you "Lady" cuz that's what you are. The mare nodded her head. Shane just shook his head as he patted her neck. He took care of her like she was a child. He rubbed her down, gave her oats and apples and she repaid him by taking him on the most thrilling rides he'd ever been on.

It was always wild excitement riding her, never the same, and he was always amazed by what she could do. She never let him down; was always ready to run and run fast. They spent many a night out under the stars. He never had to hobble her because she wouldn't run off. Better than a dog, she'd always let him know when something was around in the dark that might be dangerous. If something did show up, all he had to do was climb up on her back and they'd ride outta there. She could see in the dark. There was nothing out there that she couldn't outrun. He started teaching her tricks. It was as if she liked doing things for Shane, wanting only to please him.

Shane taught her to come when he whistled, fetch almost anything, pick a pocket, count, nod her head for yes, shake it for no, back up, lay down, and bow.

He even taught her to play hide and seek......! Lady usually won that game because Shane figured she would cheat and peek. Surely it couldn't be because he smelled like 'horse' himself! There was no limit to Shane's amazement of God's infinite grace and love that He would give him such a wonderful gift.

Early one morning, a couple months later, Shane rode down to Salida just to have a look see. While there he heard there was going to be a big horse race that day. Folks came from miles around to watch or enter their horses. Miners, loggers, railroad men, as well as ranchers would be there entering their horses or betting on other horses. People came from Cotopaxi, Sargents, Garfield, Alamosa, Bonanza, Gunnison, Westcliffe and other places within a two-day ride.

The entry fee was $2.00 with local merchants donating prizes and the bank matching the registrations to make up the first place purse. Shane figured he would enter Lady to see how she held up in a contest.

The race would be twenty miles long around a loop that ran west for five miles to Poncha Springs then turned north for a few miles, then east, and finally back to town. Seventy-three riders signed up for the race. There were expensive horses imported from back East to the Wet Mountain Valley that were bred to run. They had raced many times before and had won big races in New Mexico, Texas and Kentucky.

Beautiful horses, no doubt about it, but none of them looked like his mare. There was just something different about her that he couldn't explain.

Several of the racers and owners told Shane that he had a beautiful horse and asked if he wanted to sell her. He said there wasn't enough money in the world to get him to part with her. One of the men told him his mare didn't have a chance against his thoroughbreds, and did he care to place a bet on it if he had any faith in his horse. Shane asked how much, and the man said one thousand dollars. Shane told him he didn't have that much money. The man said he didn't figure he did.

All riders were given a number, told the route, and the rules. The course was well marked and spotters were situated at several places to make sure no one took a short cut or cheated. It was generally understood that the riders would all be close enough to each other that if someone did take a short cut, he would be seen and disqualified. The rider who passed all the checkpoints and was the first one back in town would be declared the winner. The last checkpoint was about eight miles out of town and once past this last spotter, it was a straight shot back into town.

Shane decided to wear a bright red neckerchief for the race so each checkpoint lookout wouldn't miss him as he went by. This would prove very fortuitous for him, even lifesaving.

The riders were lined up at the starting point in front of the saloon. The street was only wide enough for six riders so there were twelve or thirteen rows. The ones in the back were at a disadvantage but everyone had agreed it would be insignificant in a twenty-mile race that would take an hour or more to run. There was a draw to establish who got the positions in the first three rows and Shane was not one of these. He was well back in the pack about row nine but he was on the outside and not confined to the inside of the pack.

The starting gun went off and immediately a thick cloud of dust arose with no one seeing anything. Shane just hung on and his mare streaked through the cloud passing riders like they were statues. Shane closed his eyes against the thick dust and held his breath as long as he could. When he could hold his breath no longer, he opened one eye slightly to try to get his bearings. He noticed there was no dust at all. He was out in front of the pack already! He looked back and saw a few riders out in front of the pack and a huge dust cloud billowing up into the sky. He gave the mare her head and the gap between the next few riders grew wider and wider.

Back in town, it took several minutes for the dust to settle. The race officials had retired to the saloon to wash the dust out of their throats. The first riders wouldn't be back for a while and there was no sense in standing out in the hot sun for all that time. They would sit in the comfort of the saloon and sip whiskey until the first rider showed up. The ladies were down the street at the hotel dining room having tea and cookies. The judges figured it would be about an hour before the first rider showed up, so they had plenty of time to enjoy their whiskey and place their bets on the outcome.

There was money passing back and forth as well as the whiskey when all of a sudden the spotter standing on the roof of the livery stable hollered down to the street.

"There's a rider comin in and whoooeee he's a comin fast!" Everyone looked at his watch. It had only been right at thirty minutes so far. "This couldn't be the first rider. He had to have taken a short cut. It's impossible for a horse to travel that far that fast," they all said. It was either that or it was just some other rider coming into town who wasn't in the race.

Shane pulled up in front of the saloon and asked if this was the finish line. The starter said, "Yeah but there's no way you can be the winner. You musta took a short cut fella, there ain't a horse alive can run that fast."

The starter was angry that someone would cheat to win the race.

"Mister, I did not take any short cuts. I passed all the checkpoints and even waved to the person stationed at each one and they waved back!"

"I don't believe ya," the official said angrily. "We'll wait for the rest of the riders to come in and the spotters to see if they'll verify your wild story. I doubt that they will though."

A few minutes later, the first spotter came in. He was stationed at Poncha Springs. The official asked if Shane had passed him.

"Yes sir," he said, "he went by me like a streak o' lightnin', and he waved as he went by and I waved back. I ain't never seen nuthin' run that fast in my life! He wuz way ahead of everbody else by a good margin."

A few more minutes went by and the second spotter rode into town. The official asked him if Shane went by his checkpoint.

"Yup, he shor did, I could scarcely believe my eyes he was goin' so fast. He went by my place faster than anything I ever seen afore. Ya got a mighty fine horse, Mister," he told Shane. The official softened a bit after that but still wasn't convinced that Shane hadn't somehow taken a short cut.

A little over thirty minutes had gone by when the next rider came in. He thought he had won the race because there was no one in front of him that he could see. He told the official he had seen Shane reach the first checkpoint but never saw him again after that. He just figured he quit and went back to town. The official told him that Shane had been here for half an hour and was claiming to have won the race.

"Have any of the spotters come in yet? I wanna' talk to 'em," he yelled.

Even after he talked to both spotters and they vouched for Shane, he still wouldn't believe he came in second place, especially by such a huge margin. His horse had never lost a race before. He was obviously upset and knew that Shane had to have taken a shortcut to get back to town so fast.

"We'll see about this when the last spotter comes in," he said angrily. "I'll bet he won't back up your story. It's impossible for a horse to be that fast."

By now, riders were coming in regularly until the last one had passed the finish line. The story got around how one horse had been in thirty minutes ahead of the second place rider and the whole town was angry that somebody would claim to have won the race but had obviously cheated. They were on the verge of stringing Shane up when the official said, "We can at least wait for our last spotter, Jim Parsons, to come in and see if he'll verify the claim. Do you wish to recant your story and admit you took a short cut?" he asked Shane.

"No sir," he said, "I did not take a short cut and Mr. Parsons will verify my story. I went by his checkpoint fair and square and waved at him and he waved back."

Everyone waited anxiously for Jim to arrive. They all knew if he said the man went by his checkpoint then he had to have traveled the entire twenty miles and would have to be declared the winner. No one believed that Jim would vouch for the young man because no horse could possibly run like that.

The crowd grew more impatient and unruly until presently Jim came riding into town wondering why everyone was lined up along the street obviously waiting with great expectation for him. He couldn't understand why his presence would be cause for such excitement.

He was summoned by the official who pointed to Shane and asked, "Did this man come by your checkpoint?" The town grew quiet as they waited for Jim to answer that he did not.

Jim looked at Shane and said; "He shor did come by me, however, he wuz a good thirty minutes ahead of the next rider. I figgered he musta took a short cut around the other two checkpoints ta git' ta me that quick, but yeah, he did come past my checkpoint. He wuz' wearin' that red kerchief. He even waved too, nice fella."

There was a hush over the town, and then gasps of disbelief, then everyone crowded around Shane shaking his hand and slapping him on the back, yelling and cheering. Something happened that day the likes of which they'd never seen before. The town was in a frenzy of disbelief and amazement at this spectacle. One of them offered Shane ten thousand dollars for the mare. Shane told him very politely the horse wasn't for sale. Another man said he would double the offer and still another offered him fifty thousand.

By the time he left Salida, Shane was offered over one hundred thousand dollars for his mare. She was not for sale at any price.

Before long, the story got around to everyone in the area and Shane became quite famous. He even had the story told to himself several months later up in Leadville by an old miner. The story was told and retold around campfires and in bars all over the country.

What Shane didn't know was there were some who wanted his horse to make money with, a lot of money. If his mare could not be had legally, then other means would be used. What he also did not know was the Syndicate was still actively looking for his horse. Soon the news of his win would reach their ears in Denver.

Early the day after the race, with $150.00 in his pocket, a $25 dollar gift certificate from the general store, a beautiful new saddle blanket for Lady, and free beer from the saloon, which Shane traded for a fancy new bridal for Lady. This has been a purty good trip he thought, as he prepared to leave. Shane loaded up and was about to head out when the livery stable owner stopped him.

"Son, I like ya, ya won that race fair and square and when folks were callin' ya a liar and ready to string ya up, you kept yer wits about ya. I think I'd better warn ya bout sumthin."

"What's that," Shane asked.

"That there horse ya got sure has started folks talkin. Most are just retellin the race and such but thar wuz a couple unsavory cusses I overheard talkin' at the saloon that I didn't like. I couldn't hear much but they sure seemed interested in yer black. I don't like the looks of it. Them are tha kind that would bushwhack their own mother! Ya best be careful headin home."

"Much obliged, I will. What'd they look like?"

"Well, one of 'em was tall and lanky with a mustache and droopy eyes. The other was kinda short, stocky built with shifty eyes. He had a scar on his nose and right cheek, scraggly beard and wore a funny lookin round hat with a short brim. He kept lookin around kinda mean like. I wouldn't doubt both got their picture posted in some sheriff's office somewheres!"

"Thanks fer the tip, I'll be sure to keep my eyes open fer trouble." Shane shook the owner's hand, mounted up and left town heading north and home.

Chapter 13

Bandits

As Shane reached the edge of town, he passed a small church. There was a horse and buggy tied to the hitching post. As he rode on by, something prompted him to turn and go back. He didn't want to, because he was anxious to get home, but he had learned to always listen to that small still voice.

He rode up, dismounted, and walked up two steps to the front door. He did not tie Lady's reins to the hitching rail on purpose. He knew she would not run off, but he felt he should leave the reins tied together over her neck just in case she needed to move quickly.

"Lord, whatever reason you had me stop, I trust your will."

With that said, he opened the door and stepped inside. He quietly closed the door as he removed his hat. When his eyes adjusted to the dim light, he stopped. It was as if someone had hit him in the chest, more accurately, in the heart. A feeling of sadness and hopelessness came over him. What he saw caused him to look up and with tears forming in his eyes; he knew what he was here for.

At a simple alter railing one step down from the communion table with a wooden cross at the front of the church, knelt a young man. Next to him, a woman of slightly younger age was holding a newly born baby. The man was softly praying as the mother nursed their child.

Shane walked down the center aisle as quietly as he could but without much success for someone of his size. The couple turned, and Shane could see both had tears in their eyes. The young man stood, wiped his eyes and smiled.

"May I help you, sir?"

"Howdy, pardon me for barging in, are you the parson?"

"Yes, I am. I'm Tim Swenson and this is my wife Amanda and our daughter, Rachel."

"Pleased to meet ya, Parson. Now, this may sound a little strange but as I was goin by, the Lord held me up and told me to give you this." With that, Shane handed him $50 and the $25 dollar gift certificate, which he signed over. The young pastor looked at the gifts, looked at his wife who had started to cry again and dropped to his knees, bowing his head. "Heavenly Father, I humbly ask Your forgiveness for doubting You. Never again will I doubt Your Word or Your love. You truly are my provider." When he finally looked up, Shane was gone.

Little did Shane know, the young pastor was about to give up; go back home and work in the mines of West Virginia. He also didn't know the young family had very little food left. Tim bowed his head again, "Father, bless that man. Send your mighty angels to protect him. In Jesus' name I ask it, Amen."

As Shane rode out of town, he thought about what the livery stable owner had said. So, out loud he prayed, "Lord, Your Word says that even though I may walk in the midst of trouble You will preserve my life. You'll stretch out your hand against my enemies and it looks like I might have some. Thank You Lord, I ask that you give me wisdom on how to proceed. In Jesus name I pray, Amen!"

While Shane had been praying, something caught his eye. Lady had one ear cocked forward as usual but the other had been cocked to the rear as if she was listening to him...now what do I make of that, thought Shane. I'll have to watch those ears the next time I pray and see what she does.

Shane chuckled to himself, leaned forward in the saddle; slightly squeezed his knees, and Lady took off.

A couple hours later, as the sun began to set behind the snow capped mountains; Shane rode into a dense stand of aspen and made camp. The sky showed no signs of pending weather so he didn't construct a shelter. Just as well, tonight he wanted to be able to hear and move quickly.

Shane took his saddle off and let Lady graze nearby as he prepared to eat the cold supper he had packed before leaving town. He thought it best not to build a fire. He could not put his finger on it, but he had a feeling that something was not quite right. Shane said a silent prayer that the Lord would watch over him and Lady. He then covered up with his blanket, using his saddle as a pillow; his pistol within quick reach and fell into a light sleep.

Sometime later, Shane suddenly came awake with a start, automatically reaching for his already cocked pistol in one fluid motion. That's when he noticed Lady was standing over him with her head next to his. Shane grinned, scratched under her chin and slowly looking around. Because the moon had set, an inky blackness seemed to swallow up all but the strongest starlight. Shane knew Lady sensed something. Either known or unknown, it meant danger. Moving slowly and quietly, Shane crawled from his blanket and crept off into the dense part of the Aspen grove. Lady quietly followed, still on the alert. Shane knelt beside a double trunk of an old aspen and slowly began to scan the area for any sign of movement. The first few sweeps revealed nothing, but as each sweep ended, he would look at Lady, yep, still on alert. He trusted her God given senses more than his, so he continued to look and listen.

Shane had learned a trick some time back from an old mountain man on how to see in the dark. When searching for something moving or stationary; never look too long right at one point. Instead, use your peripheral or side vision. It takes a little practice but once mastered will allow someone to spot moving objects and even some that aren't. He knew that if he stared at an object long enough it would eventually seem to move. By looking out of only the corner of his eye, he was able to catch the real movements, if there were any. Periodically, Shane had practiced this technique and he employed it now. Squatting behind the aspen, he patiently searched the darkness.

A half hour passed. Suddenly there was the faintest of sound. Lady's head turned in the direction of the sound. Then, Shane's patience paid off. In the trees closest to where he had made camp, he saw movement. Two dark shapes crept slowly toward his campsite. Shane stiffly stood to get the blood flowing back into his cramped legs. He was well hidden, so when the two men stopped and started to draw their pistols, his deep voice piercing the darkness gave them quite a start.

"If either of you moves one more inch, both of you will die"!

Both thieves froze in mid-movement; knowing from the tone of the voice there would be no second chance. Neither said a word, what could they say; each was at the mercy of this man with steel in his voice and a cunning they had not known before.

"Put yer right hand on top of yer head, unbuckle yer gun belts with yer left hand and let 'em drop.

They both followed his directions without hesitation.

"Now, put both hands deep into your front pockets. Turn around very, very slowly facing the other

way and take three steps forward." The two hesitated,

"Do It Now!"

They did!

"Now, slowly, sit down keeping your hands in your pockets." When the two were seated, Shane came up behind them and retrieved their gun belts. "Now, take yer hands outta yer pockets and carefully remove your boots, remembering to also slowly remove the knife each of you has hidden there. After removing your boots, put the knife in one and toss both behind you."

Just then, the short one, whose name was Pogue, one of Blonger's henchmen, made an attempt to throw his knife. He gave a yelp of pain as Shane shot the knife from his hand. From then on the two did as they were told. "Now, git up and start walkin south."

"What! Are you crazy, we can't...." a shot rang out with the bullet grazing the tall thief's right ear, taking a small piece with it. "Augggg, you blowed ma ear off!"

"Not yet, keep talkin' and I will" Shane quietly replied. "Legally, I should hang you both for attempted murder and horse stealin', but I'm gonna' let you go and hope you learned that stealin' ain't only a crime but is also breakin' a couple of God's commandments, "Thou shalt not steal or kill! You may think you can get away from man's justice but you can never ever get away from God's justice."

"Now, START WALKIN SOUTH! I'll be watchin' you longer than you think, so don't try ta double back and bushwhack me, that's if you don't wanna be bear bait. Remember this, I coulda killed ya both. I'm givin' ya a second chance ta turn from a life of crime and make somethin' of yerselves. If you try somethin' like this again, there will be no third chance. "NOW GIT!""

With that, both men started walking south. The short one turned his head to look behind him then abruptly stopped. "Don't stop you idiot, ya wanna git shot?" the tall one said. His name was Slim Hicks.

"There ain't nobody there, he's gone!"

"What!" said Hicks as he stopped and turned to look. "Well, I'll be a... just then a shot rang out, kicking up the ground right between the feet of Hicks. "Oh hell! Lets git' moving afore he shoots ma big toe off!"

At that, both thieves broke into a fast trot, as best they could, with only their socks to protect their feet.

Shane chuckled to himself as he holstered his pistol. He then went back to Lady, jumped up on her bare back and took off in a southeasterly direction. He had put a halter lead on the mare but actually he didn't need it. Lady responded instantly to Shane's slightest pressure from his knees or his position shift. She seemed to know what he wanted of her.

As Shane and Lady rode quietly through the darkness, the mare seemed to sense more than see where she needed to place her hooves. *Man,* thought Shane, *I bet Lady could sneak up on a mounted Indian if need be.* Shane tried to remember where the best place would be to 'check up' on his two bootless thieves. He didn't trust the short one. Then he remembered, there was a shallow draw up ahead that would give him a good field of view from the top. When he arrived, he slid from Lady's back, rubbed her head and ears and spoke quietly, reassuring her that everything was going to be all right. Lady nuzzled Shane's neck then suddenly jerked her head up, ears cocked forward. Sure enough, here came the two, walking slowly, arguing between themselves.

"...and I say we double back and kill that guy, nobody gits the drop on me and lives to tell about it",

Pogue growled. "Well, maybe nobody gits the drop on you and maybe they jest did, but I like livin and that gent back thar' ain't human. There's sumthin strange bout him and that horse o' his. I say we cut our losses and keep headin south till daylight, then go back and look fer our horses."

"Nope! I'm goin back, my future depends on me gittin that black and your goin with me, got it?"

"Ok, Ok, but I ain't likin it," Slim grumbled.

Just then, a shot rang out that took Pogue's little right toe off. "Augggg, I'm hit! Why, you dirty son..." another shot rang out right beside his other foot.

"I ain't dirty and I ain't yer son neither. Now, git' goin! This time I would suggest you don't stop!"

"What about my toe!"

"That's yer problem. I told ya ta keep goin and not look back. Apparently, ya don't understand plain English. Next time, that bullet goes between yer eyes. With that, Shane silently melted into the darkness.

As the two robbers slowly made their way to where they had left their horses, Pogue was in a foul mood. He had failed again and Blonger was not going to be pleased. Pogue knew he could not return empty-handed. He needed a plan.

Shane returned to his campsite, saddled Lady, took the two pistols, stowed them in his saddlebags, tied on his bedroll and mounted up. As he rode northward, Shane pondered what he had heard one of the bandits say about Lady.

Upon arriving home he hugged his mother and handed her a hundred dollars.

"Son, did you rob a bank or sumthin?" his dad joked.

"No Dad, I won it fair and square in a horse race. She's the fastest critter on four legs I ever saw."

"I know Son, we already heard about the 'Great Race'."

"Yer kiddin, I just won a couple days ago."

"No, a neighbor came through yesterday and told the whole story. How the town folk wuz about to string you up before the final spotter came in and verified you wuz tellin the truth. The way he told it, made it seem like there will never be anything so fantastic ever to happen again in his life time!" At that, all laughed and began to bombard Shane with questions about the race. Shane was happy to tell the story; he just left out the part about the two thieves. No need in worrying his folks. What would have been perfect was if his wonder horse could talk. Being a female, she would have done all the talking and that would have suited him just fine. He did learn that the fellow, who thought Shane had cheated, had lost a lot of money on bets he had placed on his own horse. Word was he was still angry at losing. Shane just shrugged and figured that's what you get for betting on a sure thing that wasn't a sure thing!

Chapter 14

Steve Englert

One morning Shane decided he would ride up north and visit with Steve Englert. In addition to his place just north of Ben's place, Steve had a beautiful piece of land up on the backside of Buffalo Peaks. He had over a thousand acres of choice land along the top of the range. It was an unbelievable view from the front door of his cabin. Steve built it up against and partially into a sagebrush-covered hill near a small patch of Aspen. Two giant Ponderosa pine trees stood between the cabin and the meat shed. To the west of the meat shed stood the barn. A thirty-acre park surrounded the buildings on three sides and was overgrown with buffalo grass. A clear mountain stream came off the hill to the east and passed within a hundred feet of the front door. Beaver ponds dotted the meadow below the house and down the canyon. To the east of the cabin was a huge granite mountain range that extended fifty miles to the north. It was but a day's ride along the top of this range to Leadville. To the south was a black timbered ridge and beyond this was another large mountain park.

Elk came out into this high mountain park every evening to feed. In the winter, before the snow got too deep, hundreds of elk would be in this park as well as the one Steve lived in. It was common to look out the window of the cabin a few feet away and see elk bedded down. There were a couple herds of bighorn sheep living up here too. There was one huge old ram that Steve called Elmer. He'd been watching him for years, and he was endowed with a curl and a half.

After checking the lay of the land, Shane rode up in front of the porch and hollered, "Hello the cabin," but no one answered. He swung down off Lady and with one hand on his pistol, opened the door slowly and looked inside. Seeing no one, he went in and put some coffee on.

When he returned to the porch, he saw Steve fishing the beaver ponds at the lower end of the meadow. He sat down in one of the chairs on the porch and gazed out into the untrespassed sanctity of this high mountain wilderness.

This was home to the bighorn, grizzly, wolverine, elk, deer, mountain lion and timber wolf. Few white men had ever set foot on any of this ground.

He looked down the valley to the south and could see Mount Ouray with its huge granite bowl facing the morning sun. Across the pass to the east was Methodist Mountain, the northern tip of the mighty and impregnable Sangre De Cristo range. From the top of this, you could look down into Salida or to the south into the San Luis Valley. The Continental Divide started somewhere in Canada and extended all the way to Mexico. Thousands of square miles of virgin wilderness had never seen the footprint of a white man nor felt the blade of his axe. Huge endless tracts of timber, consisting of spruce, fir and pine, broken up by patches of aspen gave the scenery a crisp light green color in summer and wild splashes of brilliant red and gold in the fall. Only an infinite Creator could have created all this and Shane loved what He had created, continually thanking Him for it.

While Shane was lost in thought, Steve came around the corner of the cabin. "Howdy, pilgrim, ain't seen ya in a good long while. Hope you had the sense to put the coffee on." Steve stepped upon the porch and they shook hands.

"Good to see ya agin, lad. You've growed some since tha last time I seen ya. Where ya been all these years?"

"Been to school back East," Shane answered. "Sure didn't like it there, could hardly wait to get back. Where's young Taylor?"

"He's off fishin' in Florida with his mother, stayed down there this summer to catch some sharks. Caught that one and brung it last time he wuz here." He pointed to a huge round set of multi-rowed teeth nailed to the front door of the cabin.

"I wondered what the heck that thing was," said Shane. "Looks like it could bite a man plumb in two."

"That one won't be bitin' nobody again," Steve asserted. "Come on in and set a spell while I put these fish on to cook."

Steve filled his pipe, lit it and began to prepare the trout he had just caught. "Got some beans that's been simmerin since mornin. I throwed in some wild onions and a few dried chilies. Should taste purty good by now. Jest gives me time ta put the finishin' touches on things and we can dig in."

"Well, by all means, don't let me keep a gourmand from his diligent endeavors of culinary wizardry."

"Whut? Them Easterners teach ya them fancy words? I ain't fer certain, but did ya jest give me a compliment or insult me?"

Shane laughed and said, "A compliment of the highest order."

"Well, thanks!.... I think."

Shane went back out on the porch to watch the sun go down over this magnificent wilderness wondering how anything could be so beautiful and so unending in its grandeur. There was always something wild and breathtaking to look at, things with such splendor and majesty that his senses were overwhelmed. He looked up the hill to the east of the cabin and saw a grizzly cross a small clearing about four hundred yards away.

"Steve, we got company."

Steve came outside and Shane pointed to the bear.

"Yeah, been hangin' around here for several years," Steve replied casually. "His tracks are on the hill right behind the cabin; wuz here last night. Come on, I'll show ya. Ya ain't never seen nothin like this afore."

They walked around to the back and Steve pointed to a huge set of tracks that looked like a giant man had walked there in bare feet, but no man had claws that left holes like that. The paws were longer than Shane's boot and quite a bit wider.

At the front of each track were four holes where the claws had sunk into the soft earth. He had passed within twenty yards of the cabin. Shane put his index finger into one of the holes and it went all the way to his knuckles.

"He'll go twelve, maybe thirteen hundred pounds. He's over eight feet tall, Seen his territorial markin's on several trees round the neighborhood. Gave ma horse quite a stir last night. Didn't bother nuthin though. I named him Big Paw."

This was the biggest wild animal track Shane had ever seen. He could hardly believe the size of the claws. "He could cut a man to pieces with those claws," he said.

"Yeah, I reckon he could," Steve agreed. "I been kinda keepin' an eye out now that he's come so close. Ya never knowed about a griz, they jest got a mean streak in 'um and don't care who knowed it."

The two men went back into the cabin and ate supper. Shane cleaned the dishes as Steve filled his pipe with fresh tobacco, lighting it with a burning twig from the stove. After the dishes were cleaned, they retired to the porch. Steve hung the lantern on a nail so they could have some light to see by. It brightened the darkness a good fifty feet in a semicircle in front of the cabin. Steve puffed on his pipe and they talked until the moon came up and brightened the night, so he blew out the lantern. They spoke quietly, listening to the sounds of the wilderness after dark. Shane told Steve about school and what the East was like. He talked about his mare and how she could run and Steve agreed he came out on the good end of that deal.

Shane related the race Lady had run in Salida and what happened as he headed home.

"Well, if'n it been me, I'd gone ahead and shot um both," Steve said.

"Yeah, well, I just couldn't bring myself to do that. I wanted to give both a second chance."

"Well, there is some folks don't deserve a second chance". Shane started to let it pass but something kept tugging at his heart not to let it.

"Steve, you may be right about some not deserving a second chance, but where would we be if God had decided no one gets a second chance?"

There was silence between them for a while then Steve said, "Sonny, you got a point there, think I got to chew slowly on that one fer a while, so's I don't choke on it." That got a laugh from both.

"Steve, the God I know is not only a God of love and mercy, but also a God of second chances. All we have to do is believe in His Son, Jesus Christ, and do what He taught. There really is nothin complicated or hard about it."

"Well, I knowed I sure have had a lot ah second chances or I wouldn't be here now. You say it all hinges on this here Son of God called Jesus?"

"You got it."

"Well, it looks like yer gonna be given me a whole lot more ta chew on. Guess I'm gonna have ta put my store bought teeth in!" Shane laughed and shook his head.

Steve remarked that he had heard rumors about the railroad coming to the mountains. "That'll open this country up and bring trouble with it. They'll have folks runnin' all over this land with gold fever, diggin' up the ground and leavin' a helluva mess and iffin they don't find nutin there selves, they try's ta steal it from others!

There's been some strikes already and lotsa folks gittin' interested in these parts. I give em ten years afore they have this country purty much ruint."

Shane felt a twinge of despair at these words. The last thing he wanted to see was his beautiful wilderness ruined. He had seen where miners had been. They left huge scars where they dug up the earth. When they were done, they just moved somewhere else and dug up the earth again. They had no concern for the beauty of this land, not to mentions the damage done by strip mining and massive erosion. All they were concerned with was getting the gold any way they could. Neither Shane nor Steve had much use for the miners, especially Steve.

Shane heard a story about a miner who tried to take a knife to Steve in Granite, a small town up river about five miles from the cabin. The story was that Steve tried to back out of the fight, but the man just kept pushin until he stabbed Steve in the upper lip, cutting clean through and knocking out Steve's front teeth in the process. By the time that fight was over, Steve had broken both of the guy's arms, one of his legs, and some of his ribs. He cut off one of the man's ears and made him chew on it. Then he broke his jaw! After that, nobody ever bothered Steve and nobody came close to his property unless invited.

They had about run out of things to talk about. They were sitting in the moonlight when a herd of elk came into the park beyond the timbered ridge. There was one old bull in the herd whose rack shined like polished ivory in the moonlight. His yellow hide reflected the light and glistened like gold. You could count the points on his antlers with the naked eye. There were seven on each side and easily six feet long.

"Been up here for the last ten years that one," said Steve. "He just keeps gittin' bigger and older. Been a seven by seven for the last five years. Afore that he was a magnificent six by six. When he dies, I'll nail his horns to the porch. Don't wanna shoot 'im though. Heck ya couldn't chew the gravy much less the meat. He'd be tuffer'n a old boot hangin' on an outhouse door." They both got a laugh out of that one.

"Ah, Steve, ya do have a way with words. Is it because ya go so long between spells of no one ta converse with or do ya just store up all these witty one liners fer your friends?"

"You got it, Bub, just fer edjacated guys like you." That caused another round of laughing until the coyotes began their nightly singing on the ridge above the cabin. The two men sat listening to the music. From somewhere on the timbered ridge between the cabin and the elk, a hoot owl sounded off.

Then way off to the South, a wolf howled, and a few seconds later another one answered, and then all was quiet. "Guess we know whose boss of these woods," Shane said.

"That ain't necessarily so," answered Steve. "Thar's tougher animals out there that don't make no noise. The wolverine is probly the toughest animal I ever seen. One winter I wuz over on the Black and watched this pack of wolves bring down an elk calf in the deep snow. Thar wuz five wolves fightin' and scratchin' over this meal. A wolverine walked into the middle o' the fray and took it away from all them boys. There wern't much of an argument neither. Those wolves just sorta got up and left. I watched the wolverine eat his fill, growl a couple times and wander off. Within seconds the wolves' wuz back. Saw bout the same thing with a griz on Waugh Mountain a few years back, too. Wuz early spring and the griz musta just come outta hibernatin. He wuz eatin on one ol' Tom's cows that didn't make it thru the winter. A wolverine come in and run that bear off. A good fight that time but the wolverine won. Never seen such toughness in a critter so small. Hard ta trap too, seem to have some magic about 'em when it comes to tearin' up a trap line and makin' off with the bait. Ya gots to be real slick to bag one o them critters. Ya got to cover yer gloves with scent when ya set the jaws and never touch em again with bare hands. Put it down careful like and chain it to sumthin purty stout. Do this on a night when it snows so it covers yer trap. The next day git a stick 'bout ten feet long and poke the end of it into some drippins from a dead duck that ya been hangin' in the sun fer a week or ten days. Reach over yer trap with this stick and put a few drops around where yer trap is. Don't ever git within ten feet of the trap after it snows on it. The wolverine'll cut yer tracks and follow em to where he smells the scent and won't see no tracks goin' to the trap and he'll go take a look-see. Then ya got 'im!"

It was getting on late into the night and time for bed. Shane walked out to the shed to check on Lady and give her some oats. Steve's horses crowded their way in so he gave them some, too. On his way back to the porch, he looked up at the stars, as a wolf howled on the ridge behind the cabin. A shiver went down his spine as he stepped through the door and latched it behind him. He wondered if the wolves would bother the horses so he checked his rifle in the corner. It was a Spencer repeater that he bought from a gunsmith in Boston, a forty-caliber, lever action that shot seven times before reloading.

Steve had the old standby fifty-caliber Hawken muzzleloader that only shot one time before reloading, but it killed whatever Steve aimed it at. Shane rolled his bed out on the floor next to the stove and crawled inside. He blew out the lantern and lay there in the darkness.

The next thing he knew Steve was nudging him awake with the toe of his boot.

"Hey, pilgrim, ya gonna sleep the rest o' the day? We got us some huntin' ta do. It's a good day to kill a bull."

It was not yet sunup but starting to get light outside. Steve already had the coffee on. Shane rolled out of his bed and pulled his boots on. It was cold in the cabin causing Shane to shiver as he buttoned his wool shirt. Fortunately, Steve had just finished building a fire in the heat stove. He had two stoves, the smaller one to cook on and the larger one to heat the cabin.

Steve grabbed up his Hawken and quietly opened the door and stepped out onto the porch. He looked down toward the creek and saw, standing in the willows, four elk; one was a young spike bull. He had horns about a foot long, still partially covered with velvet. It was about a two hundred yard down sloping shot.

Steve put the barrel into a crook of one of the posts that held up the porch, took careful aim, allowed for the drop and windage, took a deep breath and gently squeezed the trigger. The morning silence was split by the deafening roar of the Hawken.

Smoke from the shot obscured the view but after a few seconds, Steve could see the bull thrashing on the ground. In a few seconds, he lay still. The other elk tore up the patch of willows in their effort to be somewhere else.

"Well, thars meat on tha' table," said Steve. Let's have us some vittles first then go take care o' that critter."

After breakfast, they cleaned the dishes and walked down the hill to where the bull lay dead. The bullet went in just behind the front shoulder. Shane took hold of one of the hind legs and held it while Steve began the task of gutting out the elk.

"Here's supper tonight. We'll have steak tomorrow after it's had a good chance ta cool. Go fetch the paint so we can hoist this critter and git the hide off."

Shane went to the barn and got Steve's horse; a beautiful brown and white pony he traded an Indian in South Park for a pistol and a hand full of bullets. He put a saddle on, grabbed a rope and led the paint down to the willows where Steve had removed the legs and head off the bull with his axe.

He tied one end of the rope to the saddle horn and threw the other end over a limb. Steve tied that end to a strong pole he put through the tendons on the animal's back legs and Shane led the paint forward to hoist the animal into the air. When the front shoulders were off the ground, Steve tied the pole to the limb with a shorter piece of rope and untied his good lariat.

"Just let the paint loose, she won't run off," Steve said. "Gimme a hand with this hide."

They found the Hawken's lead ball just under the skin of the ribcage on the opposite side from where it went in. Steve made a small incision and took out the flattened ball. Looking at the lead slug, Steve chuckled and said, "Died from lead poisonin best I kin figger! I kin melt this down, run it through tha press and use it again. So far I kilt six critters with this here bullet."

"Steve, I've heard of frugal people but you take the cake!"

"Cake! Who's got cake? I shornuf' could go-fer some ah that pound cake your ma makes. Boy, that cake would give a wolverine a nice disposition,. . at least fer five minutes or so. Augh, I ain't got time ta daydream bout no cake I ain't got and I ain't gonna git no how. Even if I wuz gonna git some, which I ain't, so don't be botherin' me bout' it no more!"

Shane just walked off shaking his head. He didn't see Steve grinning.

Steve cut the front quarters off, while Shane removed the backstrap from each side of the backbone, producing two pieces of meat as big around as his fist and about two feet long. He held a piece in each hand and said, "Here's vittles fer three, four days."

Shane cut two poles about ten feet long to make a travois to haul the meat to the meat shed. He tied the hide between the two poles, placed all the meat on the hide and carried it all in one trip.

After they had the meat secured in the shed and the poles removed from the saddle, Shane untied the hide and laid it out on the ground. Steve climbed onto the paint and returned to the willows. Shane wondered what he forgot. Steve returned in a few minutes dragging the bull's head at the end of his rope.

"What did you bring that thing up here for?" asked Shane.

"Need the brains to tan the hide and his buglers is ivory. Makes nice baubles fer fancy women outta them things. Can trade 'em for powder and lead."

"His buglers are made of ivory?" Shane asked incredulously. "Of all the elk I've kilt, I never knew they wuz worth anything."

"The fella I trade 'em to in town tells me the women back East pay a fancy price fer these." Steve remarked as he held them out for Shane's inspection.

Steve dragged the hide into the shed as Shane rolled the two pieces of ivory over in his hand studying them intently.

"We'll leave the heart and liver in the shed today to cool and eat 'em fer supper tonight," Steve said. "We can cut the rest of the meat tomorrow. Wanna take a ride up on top of the peaks today and look around?"

"Sure, lemme throw a saddle on Lady and I'm ready to go," answered Shane.

"Ya oughta consider spendin' the winter up here with me." Steve said as they rode up the sagebrush hill behind the cabin. "Young Taylor's gonna' stay with his ma and go to school in Florida and I'd enjoy some company."

"Ya mean stay up here, git snowed in, and have ta listen ta yer snorin' all winter? I really like ya Steve but yer snoring sometimes borders on cruel and unusual punishment! That's why no bears come around yer cabin, they're scared off by tha cacophony of noise comin from inside!"

"Look, Bub, iffin' I'm that hard to git along wit ya can jest sleep on tha roof!"

"Ok, Ok, I guess I can stand yer symphony of sounds if you can stand my cookin' and preachin. I'll need to ride down and check with the folks so they won't think I wuz eaten by yer pet bear. Besides, I need to see if they need me for anything. I could do that tomorrow and try to be back in three er four days."

"Good, I'll have that hide tanned and the meat cut up by tha' time ya git back. I'll even whittle ya a pair of earplugs! Now, ain't I nice? By the way, what be that thar cakaphony ah noise ya mentioned?

Shane just laughed and said, "It'd take too long to explain and I still don't think you'd get it.

"Yeah, well I'm gonna look it up just as soon as I learn how ta spell it."

"Well, it's sort of a compliment to your multi-faceted individuality and inner talents."

"Awright, thar ya go agin! Thanks, I think, fer the compliment but I'll have ya knowed my whatchamacallit indivigel whatever and innards is jest fine!"

Shane had to grab Steve's shoulder to keep from falling over, he was laughing so hard. When he caught his breath, he turned and looked at Steve.

"Brother, I love ya like my own dad, you are one of a kind, and God don't make junk. If you only knew how pleased He is and how much He loves you."

Chapter 15

Bad Attitude

They mounted up and rode through a patch of Aspen as they headed for the top of the range. They'd gone about a quarter mile through a stand of tall Engelmann Spruce, with Steve in front, when the paint snorted and came to a sudden stop. She was real nervous and hard to control and Steve was having a time staying on board. He was half in the saddle, half out when they heard a roar that sounded like the gates of hell were ripped from their hinges and some unspeakable demon had been loosed upon the earth. Shane saw a flash of brown coming down the hill in full charge toward Steve.

"GRIZZLY!" Steve yelled, as the paint, in a complete panic, wheeled and bolted down the hill with Steve hanging on with his left hand on the horn and his left foot in the stirrup. His right hand and foot were dangling uselessly in space as he tried to regain his balance and pull himself back up into the saddle before he was knocked off by a passing branch. He was turned completely around and could see the bear charging down the hill after him. He knew, if he was thrown from his horse, it was all over. They went down through the trees with the grizzly hot on their tail; the paint completely out of control. Then a branch caught Steve on the right shoulder, but instead of knocking him to the ground, it helped spin him around enough that he was able to pull himself back into the saddle, grab the reins, and get the horse under control before it ran into a tree and killed them both.

Steve kept the horse headed downhill because he knew the griz could outrun them uphill. He came out into a large park and ran full speed across to the other side, when he noticed the bear was not on his tail anymore. It stayed in the timber just on the other side of the park less than a quarter mile away.

Steve took the Hawken out of the scabbard in case the bear decided to charge. They sat there watching each other for a few minutes until the bear turned and ambled down the hill out of sight. A few minutes later, Shane came out into the upper end of the park, his rifle resting across the front of his saddle, cocked and ready. They rode towards each other. When they were within hearing distance, Shane shouted, "Man, I had no idea you could ride fancy like that. Do ya think ya could teach me that trick?"

"You bet, the next time we see that bear, I'll tell 'im ta chase you, not me!"

"That was Big Paw, wasn't it?"

"Yup, he shor is startin' to wear on ma nerves, either he's gonna have ta move on or we're gonna tangle one day."

Shane looked up and thanked the Lord that Steve and his horse were not hurt.

Steve took out his pipe, knocked out the ashes, and filled it with fresh tobacco. He lit it up, took a couple of puffs, smiled, then said, "Well, let's git goin, funs over."

Shane just grinned, shaking his head.

When they came out on top above timberline, they could look into South Park and examine the wide expanse of Bayou Salado. Pikes Peak, with its snowcapped summit, loomed into the sky almost a hundred miles to the east. To the south were the Buffalo Peaks still covered with snow. They rode in that direction and cut tracks in the snow where many large animals had crossed. The path was as wide across as the Arkansas River and was made that morning.

"Buffler," said Steve. "Couple hunderd head I 'spect. Probly over in Salt Creek country by now. Plenty o' grass over there for 'em to winter on." A cold wind started to blow so they rode down off the top of the ridge to escape its bite. They rode for a patch of dark timber ahead. Once inside the rectangular shaped stand of Engelmann Spruce, they noticed movement in the shadows. Elk were getting up all around them. Shane noticed one was having trouble getting to its feet. He rode towards it and saw its bed was covered with blood. The elk was a young cow and had a terrible wound on one of its hindquarters and on the throat.

"Wolves musta got after 'er," said Steve. "She'll not last long, better put 'er out of 'er misery."

The elk stood shakily with its head down. Shane took aim with his rifle and put a bullet between its half-closed eyes. It crumpled to the ground and lay there kicking for a few second; then was still. The rest of the herd was nowhere in sight. Steve and Shane dismounted and stood over the dead cow.

"That'll make good vittles fer the crows and coyotes," Steve said. "Woulda been that anyway in a day or two, least now she don't have ta suffer no more."

They mounted up again and rode toward the Peaks to the south. The sun was high in the blue sky and out of the wind it was pleasant. They stayed along the edge of the timber winding their way down along the west rim rock of Buffalo Peaks, where they could look down on the Arkansas River a thousand feet below.

To the north, they could see the cabin nestled against the sagebrush hill. As they sat there watching, a large brown form entered the park to the east of the cabin and ambled straight for the meat shed.

"Could be trouble," Steve said. "Dang, looks like that grizzly's back! Better git down there quick!"

Carefully they picked their way through the rocks hurrying as best they could trying to get back to the cabin.

Almost an hour later, they rode into the park and found the meat shed mostly torn down and its contents strewn all over the place. Deep gashes were cut into the door where the griz had torn it from its leather hinges and then chewed chunks of wood out of it. Once inside the shed, he slashed and tore at the walls until he knocked out the entire front of the structure. He then chewed huge bites out of the meat and what he didn't eat, he scattered all around.

Steve was fit to be tied and madder than an old wet hen! Shane had never seen him so riled up. He got a taste of it this day. Steve was ready to hunt the bear down right then and there and fill him full of hot lead.

"Why do you s'pose that critter would do something like that?" Shane asked.

"Must be somethin' bout me he don't like. I knowed I shor don't like nuthin bout him! Can't figger it. Lived up here with 'em fer years and ain't had no trouble. Don't know what his problem is, he's got plenty other food. All I gotta say is he's gittin' close to havin' his hide tacked onto my wall for sure. We gotta' shoot us some more vittles now. Dagnabit!"

"Well, maybe he's just gittin old and a little grouchy like you,"

"Who says I'zs grouchy, I ain't grouchy! I ain't old neither!"

Shane laughed as he picked up the elk hide. Fortunately, it hadn't been touched, neither had the heart and liver. "Better take these into the house," Steve said. They went in and Steve put some coffee on and began to cut the heart and liver into strips for supper, mumbling the entire time about the bear, its personality, ancestors, age and even looks!

Shane's laughing, caused Steve to get even madder and more vocal about bears in general and how some folks think it's funny. When Shane finally quit laughing, he said, "When I git back, we'll go bear huntin."

"Ya got that right, Bub! "

"Besides, I ain't sure I could stand much more of yer grousin!"

"Humph," was all Steve said.

The next morning dawned cold and clear. Shane shivered as he pulled on his boots. He stoked up the stove fire then quietly opened the door and stepped out onto the porch to see what he might find in the early morning.

The mountains were full of many wild and interesting creatures and Shane never grew tired of watching them. He looked on the hill behind the cabin at the edge of the sagebrush clearing and saw a lone bull elk grazing on the yellow buffalo grass, his polished ivory antlers glistening in the morning sun. In the park beyond the timbered ridge, in front of the cabin, a herd of twenty elk were grazing along with several mule deer.

It was so peaceful and quiet Shane could not understand how people lived in a city where their lives were dominated by clamor and haste. They always seemed to be rushing somewhere trying to start one thing or finish another before the hands of the clock said it was time to stop. They seemed to be slaves to this mechanical contraption that governed every move they made from the time of birth till they drew their final breath.

Shane was lost in this particular line of thought when his attention was diverted by movement in the willows below the cabin. There on the frozen gut pile, a pair of coyotes was feeding. The trees above were full of crows and magpies and from time to time one would fly down and try to snatch a morsel of food, but the coyotes would run them off, completely uninterested in sharing their breakfast with anyone. Frost covered the ground and the blades of grass glistened like diamonds as they reflected the morning sunlight. Down on the creek, a red fox crossed one of the frozen beaver ponds. He no doubt had dined on the gut pile during the night and left when the coyotes showed up.

Shane went back into the cabin. He had to break through a layer of ice in the water bucket with his knife so he could make coffee. He poured a pot full, threw in a handful of ground coffee and set it on the stove. After checking the progress of the fire, feeding it a couple more sticks, he stepped back out onto the porch. A short time later, Steve came out and handed Shane a cup of hot coffee.

"You sure gotta nice place up here," Shane told Steve. "Don't know that I've ever seen anything so purty."

"Well, it suits me," said Steve. "Me and civilization don't git along too well; so its probly good that I stays up here and they stays down thar where we ain't in each other's way. When ya git back, we gotta' make a run to Leadville to pick up some supplies afore we git snowed in fer the winter."

"Be back as quick as I can" and with that, Shane threw the coffee grounds from his empty cup onto the frosted ground and said, "Guess I better hit the trail."

They both walked to the barn where Shane rubbed Lady's forehead, then led her out into the sunlight, threw a blanket and saddle on her back, cinched up, then tied on his saddlebags and rain slicker. "You ready to go for a ride, girl?" Lady nodded and stamped her right foot.

"That is one smart horse ya got there," laughed Steve.

"Yeah, ya keep studyin' and you'll be almost as smart as Lady one day!"

"Horse Feathers!"

Laughing, Shane said, "I'll see ya in a few days," as he swung easily into the saddle. "Keep an eye out for that pet bear o' yers. I like yer company and don't wanta find yer mangy carcass strewn all over this meadow!"

"It ain't my carcass that's gonna be strewed all over this here meadow! I ain't mangy neither!" he shouted, as he watched Shane ride out of sight, laughing. Steve smiled, "That boy has turned into one fine fella and smart ta boot. I'm sure glad he's comin back." Steve smiled then turned and went back inside to fix breakfast.

Chapter 16

Gettin Ready

After breakfast, Steve walked over to what was left of the shed and scratched his long red beard. He wondered aloud why, after all this time, this critter had changed. He'd lived up here for years and never had a run in with this bear. The thought crossed his mind that another bear had taken over the area or he may have been wounded. Whatever the reason, Steve's patience was about to run out. "Pet my foot! I'm fixin ta show ya whose pet ya are."

He collected the tools the bear had scattered and began to repair the shed. The only real damage was the door hinges and the front wall, which he could repair with a little time. What really angered him was all the meat that was ruined. The bear ate only a small part and then just chewed up the rest of it and scattered it all over the place. This meat was to have been part of their winter supply, now he would have to take time to go hunting again and then time to take care of it. He had a lot to do to prepare for winter. Once the snow set in, whatever wasn't done would have to wait till spring. He loved to hunt more than anything else, but the shed repair would take him all day. A new supply of meat to last the winter had to be put up, plus a trip to Leadville for needed supplies as soon as Shane got back, if the snowstorms would hold off. He was concerned they might not have that much time before deep snow covered the ground and the game left the high country. Beautiful as this country was, it was mostly barren of big game in the winter months. There was too much snow for them to survive. In a bad winter, the snow would be higher than the roof of the cabin. Steve was glad Shane was spending the winter with him. Thinking of Shane, Steve remembered that if the boy got in a fix or didn't know what to do, he'd always say he had to check with his Heavenly Father and see how to proceed ...er sumthin like that.

"Guess I'll give it a try, he thought, can't hurt none. Well, here goes." So, with hat in hand, Steve bowed his head,. . . then he looked up. "I don't know how to start! Lemme think. Shane just started talkin' normal like. Ok, here goes!"

"Well God, I got a potenchul problem. That dang bear done ruint our meat, not to mention what he done to my shed! I cud shor use yer help in gittin this here entire problem worked out. I been chewin' on what Shane's been sayin and I want more o' what you got ta offer, I jest ain't quite sure how ta go 'bout it. I knowed Shane said it were easy, all I got ta do is ask but that can't be all of it. Well, I seem to be diggin' that hole deeper so I'll jest say what's on my mind . . ..Help! In yer Son's name,. . . I think Shane called him Jesus, I ask it. That's all I got, thank ya fer listenin'." Oh yeah, Amen."

Steve worked on the shed for most of the day and by late afternoon had it put back together much sooner than he had expected. He fetched the hide from the cabin and began the task of tanning it. When he was young, he spent much time with the Ute Indians and learned how they prepared their hides. They used the brain of the animal, boiling it with water to form a paste, carefully working it into the skin, softening and preserving it. This process takes a long time but produced a very soft, supple material that can be used for moccasins, a coat or a pair of breeches that would last many moons. It could be made waterproof and keep out the cold of the worst blizzard.

Steve also cut thin strips to use as webbing for another pair of snowshoes to walk on top of deep snow. Thick willow branches were soaked in water and formed into a rounded frame, which the leather strips were attached to in a criss-crossed pattern. One of these frames could then be attached to the bottom of each moccasin and in this way, a man could walk on top of the snow instead of sinking up to his waist.

Steve worked late into the night on the hide and had it completed by the time the full moon was high overhead. He walked back to the cabin, hung the lantern over the stove and built a fire. There was backstrap left so he cut some slices off and dropped them in the skillet. Coffee and beans were heated up alongside. When he finished his supper, he filled his pipe and went out to stand on the porch. He liked the way Shane prayed so he said a silent prayer asking for an explanation and guidance on what to do about the bear. It wasn't so much he heard an actual voice; but all of a sudden, he knew the answer to his question, which amazed him to no end. "Now ain't that sumthin," he thought.

The bear in question was old and his time on earth was coming to an end. He had been sent to Steve so that his life could be ended quickly instead of slowly dying of starvation. Steve felt this was the way of giving the bear a dignified death and providing Steve with sustenance as well. Steve asked when he would see the bear again.

The answer came .... "When his time comes you will find his tracks on the ridge behind the cabin.." Steve was to follow the tracks until he found the animal. He was then to dismount, approach the bear on foot, and plunge his knife through the heart of the bear. The bear would die at his feet. Steve was then to use all parts of the animal that could be used.

These things he was told to do and he would comply. For some strange reason, he never doubted the power of Shane's God to protect him.

The next morning Steve was up well before dawn saddling the paint. He wanted to be on top of the ridge watching the park above the cabin to try to get an elk for their winter meat supply. Just before first light, he dismounted and climbed to the top of his lookout rock and settled into a crevice to wait for the sun to give him sight.

Slowly the dark gave way to gray dawn and then to shooting light. Just as he expected there were elk in the park. About twenty head were feeding at the edge of the timber 200 yards away. There was one great old bull, with huge antlers. He appeared to be crippled in one back leg but seemed to get around in spite of his injury.

Steve figured it must have been caused by an arrow or a misplaced slug from a Hawken. There were a couple other smaller bulls, the rest cows and calves. He picked out a small spike, took sight on his rib cage and squeezed the trigger. The quiet morning air was violated by the explosion. After the smoke cleared the rest of the elk were gone and his bull lay dead. He climbed down from his perch, mounted his horse, and rode over to the animal. In just a few minutes, he had the elk field dressed and a rope around its head dragging it back to the cabin behind the paint. He hung it in the giant Ponderosa next to the shed. He then took the saddle off the paint and turned her loose to graze.

He let the bull hang and went into the cabin to make coffee. While he waited, he took out his sharpening stone and put an edge on his skinning knife. In no time at all he could shave with that knife but a beard would come in handy keeping his face warm this winter. Besides, he thought he looked kinda handsome with a beard. And best of all, it kept stuff from falling down the front of his shirt!

When the coffee was done, he poured a cup, filled his pipe, and went to sit on the porch. He sat his cup down and went back into the cabin and grabbed a handful of jerky he had been drying. There were cords strung along the ceiling the length of the room and these were used to hang strips of meat to dry. Venison dried in this manner would last almost indefinitely. This meat was from a buck still in velvet that he had taken in late summer and the meat was now two moons old.

He returned to the porch and leaned back in his chair made of bull willow and elk hide. Gazing out over this endless expanse of unbroken wilderness, he began to plan what else must be done to prepare for the coming winter. Mostly everything was done except laying in an adequate supply of food and firewood.

Steve spent most of the day working on the elk. He skinned it, cut it into quarters, and then hung these in the shed. He cut the back straps from the ribs and hung them in the shed as well. He crushed the skull with his axe and removed the brain and wrapped it in the hide to tan the next day. He cut the buglers from the bull's upper jaw and put them on the shelf next to the two from the earlier bull. This ivory could be traded in town for almost anything; lead, powder, coffee, knives.

Jewelers made necklaces and trinkets that brought an extravagant price back east.

What he didn't trade for with ivory, Steve traded for with the gold he panned from a special spot on the Arkansas River. In a few days time he could pan all the gold he needed for a year. He typically saved this chore for late summer, when the river was shallow and the weather was warm.

When all the meat was put up, Steve cut a fourth of one backstrap off and took it to the cabin for breakfast the next morning. It was nearly sundown by now and through the door, he could see the shadow of the paint and his packhorse grazing in front of the porch. He stepped out into the dusk and led the horses back to the barn, gave both some oats, and then went to bed.

The next day the sun brought forth another typical breathtaking and beautiful morning. Sunlight glistened on frost-covered grass and a herd of bighorn grazed in the park above the cabin. Grouse were feeding in the spruce down by the creek and a mule deer buck with enormous polished antlers was standing right in front of the porch. Steve built a fire in the cook stove and put the coffee on. His sourdough biscuits would taste mighty good with fresh elk steak, beans and a little wild honey he had collected during the summer. He cut the backstrap into thin round steaks and put them into the skillet to fry in bear grease. The beans were heated in the oven next to the biscuits. This was a meal fit for a king and Steve knew of no finer vittles. Well, he wished he had some potatoes; and maybe he could find some in Leadville.

He poured a cup of coffee and quietly stepped out onto the porch while the steak was frying. He watched a wolverine work the gut pile for a few minutes and went back inside to finish frying the steak.

The biscuits were done and Steve filled his plate with hot beans and steak and sat down at the wooden table with his pan of sourdough biscuits. When his plate was empty, he took two more biscuits, covered them with honey and washed them down with another cup of steaming hot coffee. Such wonderful vittles and most of it was free and in infinite supply up here. Just the way he liked it.

He filled his pipe and headed for the barn. The horses were restless and he let them out to graze the park while he worked on the elk hide.

There was a frame built from jack pine poles in front of the shed and Steve draped the hide over it and began to cut the fat and pieces of flesh off and prepare it for tanning. This was a tedious task that took a lot of time and lasted until the sun was high overhead.

After several hours of working, it was time for a break, so, Steve went to the cabin and ate some steak left over from breakfast, wedged between a couple of his sourdough biscuits with wild honey. A cup of coffee went with him back to the shed to continue preparing the hide. He worked throughout the rest of the afternoon massaging the brain into the hide carefully covering every square inch. Just before sundown, he finished his task, took the hide back into the shed, and stretched it on a frame made of bull willow. When he was done, he filled his pipe and went to fetch the horses.

The sun was going down now and silver streaks of orange light shot up into the mottled sky. Shadows crept up the canyon toward the cabin and the buffalo grass was turning from gold to gray. The sagebrush on the hill took on a purple hue. Steve went to sit on the porch and watch the spectacle of day turn into night. It was like daybreak in reverse. The wilderness was a living entity with infinite character and personality, dependent upon the seasons, light and dark.

The measure of time was of no importance up here. Steve leaned back in his chair, put his feet up on the porch railing, and gazed out on this purple mountain's majesty. He watched as the colors changed from blues, golds, greens and reds to different shades of gray. When the valley below turned into a sea of black and there was only a thin line of orange light on the distant horizon, he went into the cabin and lit the lantern. He built a fire in the cook stove and sliced some meat from the backstrap to fry for supper. There were two biscuits left from breakfast so he put them in the oven to warm. The coffee pot went on the stove next to the skillet. In a short time, he was feasting on steak, hot biscuits and honey.

When he finished eating, he took a cup of coffee and went up on the roof to watch the stars. The world was completely void of light except for millions of sparkling emeralds in the heavens. From time to time a brilliant flash would streak across the infinite darkness. It was a source of great wonderment for him because he had not the slightest comprehension of what these were.

From somewhere on the hill behind the cabin a wolf howled, it sent a chill down his spine. At the same time, it gave him a feeling of security because it meant the encroachment of civilization was not yet imminent.

The moon was beginning to come up over the range to the east and it dulled the brilliance of the stars; but lit up the park at the same time to reveal elk feeding a short distance in front of the cabin. Steve silently watched these magnificent animals as they peacefully grazed on the buffalo grass a stone's throw from his perch. The herd was led by a huge monarch with massive antlers that stood above his head like giant tree branches. They shined in the moonlight and glistened like ivory tipped sabers. His yellow hide was almost the same color as the grass on which he fed and his black neck was the color of night. Steve stayed on the roof until the coyotes began to sing somewhere in the canyon, then he jumped down and went in to bed.

The next day was cloudy and overcast with a chill in the air. The mountaintops around the park were covered with snow clouds and from time to time, a few snowflakes fell at the cabin. Rain was falling far below in the Arkansas River Valley. Steve spent the whole day cutting meat. He cut some into steak and some into chunks that he could mix with beans and dried the rest.

Connected to the back of the cabin and dug into the hill, he had built a cellar. It kept his meat frozen in the winter and the ice he cut from the beaver ponds cooled it during the summer. He figured there was now enough meat to last for at least two moons. With Shane coming to spend the winter and considering his size, they would need a lot more meat. Steve expected him back any day now and they would need to lay in an adequate supply. They would also need to make a trip to Leadville to pick up staples like flour, beans, coffee, lead, and powder.

Shane showed up three days later. Steve was across the park in the timber cutting firewood when he rode in. Finding no one at the cabin, he deposited his saddlebags, heard the sound of an axe, and rode over to help out.

"Looks like I got back just one day too early," he said.

"Yeah, yer sense of timin' ain't so good," chuckled Steve. "But now that yer here, lasso them logs and drag um up to the cabin."

Steve had a dozen dead trees down and was working on another one. Shane unraveled his rope, threw a loop over the small end of one of the trees, dallied the other end to his saddle horn and headed for the cabin. When he got back, Steve had another tree on the ground and was chopping the limbs off. Shane lassoed another log and dragged it away. They worked most of the rest of the day and when they finished there were more than a score of logs lying next to the woodpile.

"Well, that's probly enuff work fer today," said Steve, "let's go have a bite to eat. We can cut that up in a day or two. We gotta' go to Leadville tomorrow afore the snow traps us in here." He put on a pot of coffee and began to make a batch of sourdough biscuits. Shane had brought some potatoes, wild onions and medicinal herbs back with him so he started cutting the spuds up to fry.

Steve mentioned that he was expectin' Shane to get back a few days earlier and Shane answered, "I spent a couple days cuttin' firewood for the folks and one day cuttin' meat. Then we went down to Salida and loaded up with potatoes. Yesterday, I helped Pa and Ben patch a hole in the roof. A bad wind came through and tore part of it off the day we were in town. Rained hard there. Looks like you had snow up here."

"Just a skiff here," Steve answered, "probly a half foot on top of the range. We'll be up there tomorrow and we can take us a look see."

The coffee was boiling so Steve poured them each a cup while the rest of the vittles were cooking. They sat down at the table and Shane asked, "What's been goin on since I left?"

Steve explained that he killed another bull, tanned both hides, got all the meat cut and the shed repaired. "Ain't seen the bear since you left, we'll go find him when snow falls and we git back from town."

"Man, for an old geezer, you shor got a lot done!"

"All right, thar ya go again bout me bein' old! Iffin' you'd like to step outside and go a couple rounds with my pet bear, I'll fix it up."

Shane burst out laughing, "NO THANKS! I give up, you win. You ain't that old, at least not yet!"

"Ya better believe it, Bub!"

They both went off to bed at that, with Steve mumbling somethin' Shane could not understand. It sounded like Ute Indian dialect. He figured he better learn some of their lingo, for his own safety!

The next morning they were up before dawn getting ready for their trip to Leadville. It was clear and cold when they finished breakfast. The sun was just coming up when they got to the barn. They saddled the paint and Shane's mare and took the packhorse to load with supplies. They made good time, by mid morning, they were on top of the range heading north and by noon they had arrived in Leadville.

Chapter 17

Leadville

Clouds hung low over this wild and lawless mountain town and the mud was frozen in the main street. A man could lose his life in an instant here and you had to stay on guard all the time. There were people here from all walks of life, from the wealthiest to the most desperate and everything else in between. Throngs of people crowded the streets - gamblers, miners, thugs, thieves, drunkards, escaped convicts and all other lower forms of human life. Saloons were overflowing day and night and the noise was almost deafening from all the ruckus going on.

The town had hotels, brothels, lodging houses, restaurants, lumberyards, smelting, reduction works, blacksmith shops, livery stables, jewelry stores, gambling houses, undertakers and even a few churches. Almost anything the human mind could dream up could be bought in Leadville.

Rents were high, water scarce. Everybody wore a gun. Steve and Shane rode up the street past where the new courthouse was being built and saw two hanged men dangling from the rafters. On up the street they went past St. George's Episcopal Church and heard strains of "The Old Rugged Cross" from inside. The sign out front said the pastor was Arthur Lake.

They continued up the frozen, muddy street past the Pioneer Hotel and the Carbonate Concert Hall with a sign over the door that said simply - Wine, Women and Song. On the right side of the street was the Brass Ass Restaurant, which was the most fashionable restaurant in town. Farther up the street, it made a dogleg to the right and they passed in front of a building under construction. Right next door was the Clarendon Hotel. Just a short distance from here was the general store. They pulled up in front, tied their horses to the hitching rail and went inside.

The store had rows and racks and shelves of everything and anything you could imagine. Merchandise was hanging from all roof supports as well as the roof beams. It would take forever to see, much less inventory and they traded for anything of value. Steve and Shane went through the store picking up the necessities they would need to last until spring.

They rounded up flour, coffee beans, pinto beans, a small sack of salt and a tin of ground pepper to the counter, where a man named Ollie asked, "That be it?

Steve said, "I'll be needin some terbacky, lead and powder too."

Ollie fetched the tobacco from the shelf behind him and went to a side room and returned with a can of gunpowder and a block of lead. Shane walked around the store and returned with a bag of oats and a large bottle of hot sauce. They took one more trip around the store in case they had forgot something, then each returned to the counter.

Steve took out a leather pouch from his coat, dumping its contents in front of Ollie. In the bag were ten elk teeth and some gold nuggets. Ollie took all the teeth and two nuggets to pay for their supplies.

Shane protested and tried to pay for half, but Steve wouldn't hear of it. The two men bid Ollie farewell and departed.

They tied the supplies on the pack frame of the spare horse, then covered them with heavy-duty canvas and tied it down tight. Then they rode off down the street to the front of the Golden Burro Restaurant where they tied up and went inside to enjoy somebody else's cooking for a change.

The place was abuzz with gambling, drinking and music. Steve and Shane took a table against a wall where they could look through a window and keep an eye on the horses. A young woman immediately came over to wait on them. They ordered their meal; beefsteak, beans, mashed potatoes with gravy and hot coffee, plus a shot of whiskey to warm their insides while they waited. The drinks came and as they sipped the vile liquid, loud voices could be heard, and then a shot rang out. They turned in time to see a man with a round hole in his forehead fall backwards out of his chair. The room was silent for a few moments and then returned to normal as if nothing had happened.

The dead man lay on the floor for a while before a man in a white shirt and bowtie came with two helpers and carried the dead man outside. By now, their meal had arrived along with the coffee. They ate carefully, keeping one eye on the room full of people and the other on their horses tied up outside.

When they finished eating, Shane insisted he pay for the meal, which he did, after he threatened to tie Steve backwards on his horse, which sealed the deal! They mounted up, heading out of town toward the grim and uncompromising Mosquito Range and home with low, gray clouds threatening snow any minute.

They had covered about three miles when out of a grove of trees came three men riding at them full gallop. Steve reached instinctively for his pistol and Shane drew and cocked his rifle. The three men began to shoot too soon, with several bullets whizzing past Steve's head. He drew his pistol and shot one man dead center in the chest. He fell off his horse and piled up in the snow, dead. Shane, lighting quick, took aim at the same time and emptied another saddle. And with one more quick shot there were three empty saddles and three dead men staining the blowing snow with their blood.

"Dang! That was quick shootin Son. I'm surprised we made it this far afore we had to kill somebody," said Steve matter-of-factly. Shane just shook his head, patted Lady's neck, and said nothing.

They never dismounted but kept riding, leaving the three bodies for coyote bait. Snow had begun to fall in earnest, so they rode hard to reach home before they were stranded in the deep snow. Mile after mile, through the deepening snow they went. Their progress was slowed considerably, but they kept on. They were still a good distance from home when it got dark.

The worsening snow continued to hamper their progress with each passing hour. By the time they reached the ridge they had to take to get down to the cabin, the snow was nearly up to the horse's bellies. They entered the timber where the snow wasn't quite as deep but still offered considerable resistance. They finally reached the cabin. Horses and men were completely exhausted. They barely had strength to unload the supplies, put the horses in the barn, remove their saddles, and give them some oats. When this was done, they struggled into the cabin and built a fire to thaw out.

Steve's hands shook so bad he had trouble lighting a match to start a fire. The snow continued to fall outside.

Finally, the inside of the cabin was beginning to warm up so Steve put a pot of coffee on. They crowded around the stove trying to soak up every bit of warmth they could and get the feeling back into their fingers and toes. By the time the coffee was boiling, the cabin was getting comfortable.

They took off their elk skin coats, poured coffee into tin cups, massaging the warm metal with cold hands until the feeling returned. Finally, the cold left their bones and they began to feel almost normal again.

Steve remarked, "It's a good thing we didn't decide to go to town tomorrow, we'll likely be here till spring now."

"Suits me," answered Shane, I'm thinkin' we wuz lucky to be so close to home when the hard snow hit. We coulda spent the winter in a snow bank on top of the range."

They sat around the stove soaking up heat and sipping hot coffee and chewing dried venison until the fire died down in the cook stove. Shane made a fire in the heat stove and they crawled into their beds and went to sleep.

Chapter 18

Buffler!

The sky was gray but the storm had passed by the next morning when they awoke. Steve forced the door half open with considerable effort and stepped out into snow up to his knees. He jumped off the porch into white powder up to his waist. "Never seen it snow this much at one time."

"Me neither," answered Shane, "it's a good thing it stopped when it did or we'd be tunneling around like a bunch of moles!" He leaned against the railing and gazed off down the canyon. All that was visible in any direction was a dense white blanket. Only the walls of the shed and the barn broke the monotony of the snow. To the south toward Salida, thick clouds still lingered. It gave the effect of being in a giant, soundproof room. The world was dead silent and nothing moved, as if everything was in a state of suspended animation. The scenery was pristine, unblemished, desolate and at the same time beautiful in a way misunderstood and unappreciated by civilized man. Snow scoured and cleansed the earth like a natural antiseptic. It purified the air and land. It gave a sparkle to the countryside. It was but one more dimension of the infinite wisdom of God's creation.

Steve climbed back on the porch and shook the snow out of his beard. "Won't be nobody up here botherin' us fer a few months now." He then went in to make coffee.

Shane broke a trail to the barn to check the horses. Snow had to be pushed out of the way to open the door. He led the horses out into the snow, so they wouldn't be too cooped up in the barn. They plowed through the deep powder and began to paw down to the grass that lay covered below. Shane left them to do what they could with the white stuff and went back into the cabin. Steve was making biscuits, so he went to the cellar, got some backstrap, and began to cut steak for breakfast.

As they sat eating, the earth began to tremble and the horses began to raise a commotion outside. Then a sound like far off thunder was heard. Shane jumped up and opened the door to see what had excited the horses.

All three horses were facing east with their ears cocked forward as they whinnied and stamped their feet nervously. Shane peered around the door looking up the hill where the horses had directed their attention.

By now, Steve had come to the door and was looking the situation over. As soon as he saw the boiling cloud of snow, he knew immediately what it was.

As the cloud drew nearer and the thunder became louder, the horses spooked and headed back toward the barn. Shane's heart began to beat faster and faster and still, he couldn't make his mind comprehend what he was seeing.

"Buffler!" Steve yelled and ducked back into the cabin. Moments later he appeared with the Hawken with the hammer drawn back. "We gotta' git us one o' those critters," he said excitedly. "May not git another chance afore spring."

The huge billowing cloud soon engulfed the cabin. Shane could see the shaggy beasts through the hazy mist, their long hair covered with snow and ice. The thundering herd split; half went right of the cabin and the rest went left.

Steve pointed the Hawken at the nearest animal, aiming more by sound than sight, and pulled the trigger. At the report of the 50-caliber rifle, it was as if all the volcanoes of hell erupted simultaneously when the animals panicked. They scattered and ran in all directions, kicking up the snow into such a frenzy that all vision was lost. It was like a thick fog had settled on the park and Steve thought the herd might completely trample the cabin. For a moment of time, that seemed like an eternity, the herd shook the ground and rattled the cabin as the two men waited inside for the walls to be crushed down around them. After the animals had passed by, the ground continued to shake for a good long time until the rumbling slowly faded and silence returned.

They opened the door to find the air choked with billowing snow and visibility next to nothing. Steve had no idea whether his bullet had found its mark, but he knew if he had missed, it might be a long time before they had another chance to take some meat. With snow this deep all the big game would migrate to lower ground. These buffalo were in the very process of leaving the deep snow of the high country behind. They might travel for days before they stopped.

The elk and deer would do the same thing and in a day or two, there wouldn't be anything larger up here than a rabbit or a grouse. They needed a substantial quantity of meat to last until spring and one buffalo would probably be enough with the elk they already had.

With the amount of blowing snow still in the air they couldn't see anything; so they went back into the cabin to finish breakfast. By now, the food was cold and the fire had almost gone out. Shane put more wood in the stove to warm up the biscuits and in a few moments they sat down to warm food again. By the time they finished eating, the cloud had thinned out enough for them to see.

The air was filled with snow dust and each particle sparkled with reflected sunlight and filled the air with millions of miniature rainbows. This was a sight that neither Steve nor Shane had ever seen before. The sky was alive with brilliant shimmering splashes of color as the light reflected from one glimmering particle to another. They watched this show until the snow dust settled back to earth and revealed a sky of azure blue overhead. To the south, the storm clouds were beginning to disappear over the Sangre De Cristos, leaving behind a blanket of snow in its wake.

In the park in front of the cabin where the snow was waist deep before, it was now trampled to a depth less than the width of the stock on a Hawken rifle. The buffalo cut a swath through the park and on the hill behind the cabin, a hundred yards wide!

Based on the size of the path they cleared and the amount of time it took the animals to pass the cabin, Steve estimated the herd to be close to five thousand head! They probably would have trampled the cabin if the pile of logs hadn't been there that they had piled up for firewood a few days earlier. That pile of logs was nearly as large as the cabin itself and may have saved their lives. They looked down the canyon past the barn hoping to see a dead buffalo lying in the park, but all they saw was trampled snow.

"Dang, guess I musta missed," said Steve in disgust. "Don't know how I coulda' done that with all them critters at tha end of muh gun barrel. Course, there was a lotta snow blowin and I didn't git a chance ta take careful aim like usual." Dang," he said again. "Probly won't git another chance like that again. Don't 'member the last time it wuz when I missed. My eyes must be goin bad."

"Don't dwell on it," Shane said sympathetically. "Even the best of us miss once ever few years, but if yer needin' some lessons I'd be glad to oblige ya."

Steve rolled his eyes and shook his head, but said, "You best go check the horses, and I'll go clean up the breakfast dishes."

Shane stepped off the porch and headed for the barn. He found the horses outside grazing on the grass that was now trampled but partly exposed. He walked past the corner of the stable looking down the canyon and noticed an odd shaped mound of snow. He walked over to investigate and saw the snow was soaked with blood. Kicking the mound of snow revealed a dead buffalo. He had made it as far as the barn and being mortally wounded, probably staggered and fell out of sight of the cabin.

"Steve didn't miss," Shane said to himself. "He'll be happy to know that his eyesight ain't gone bad after all."

The horses were feeding on the exposed grass, so he left them there and went to the cabin to give Steve the good news. He was just finishing the dishes and had a fresh pot of coffee on when Shane walked in.

"Horses ok?" he inquired.

"Yup, they're just fine. Those buffalo plowed up the snow pretty good," Shane answered. "Plenty of grass fer the horses now."

"Ya didn't happen to see a dead buffler down there did ya? It just ain't like me to miss like that."

"Down where?"

"Down where the buffler wuz."

"Where wuz that?"

"Down towards the crick! Where in tarnation did ya think I ment?"

"Oh, that place, well, ... as a matter of fact. . . nope, didn't see a thing down by tha creek. There might be sumthin down by the barn, can't be sure tho. Did see somethin, can't say fer sure what it wuz, could just be a pile o' snow, but it kinda resembled a dead buffalo."

Steve shot a glance at Shane, his eyes wide and exclaimed, "Really? There really is a dead buffler down there? You wouldn't be jokin' with me would ya? I knew I couldn't 'a missed, it just ain't like me to miss. Is there really a dead buffler down there?"

"Down where?"

"Where! You idgett, down by the crick!"

I told ya, there ain't nuthin down by the creek."

"Well, is thar one somewheres else?"

"One what?"

"BUFFLER!" DAGNABIT! Shane, iffin you don't give me a straight answer, I'm gonna rap this here fryin pan around yer dang head!"

"Yup, there is. Ya kilt 'im good. We best go down and fetch 'im."

"WHOOPEE!"

Steve let out a whoop and was in high spirits now that he knew his bullet had found its mark after all. He had been more concerned about missing, than doing without the meat. It would have been a serious blow to his pride, although he would have tried not to show it.

They gulped down a quick cup of coffee, grabbed the skinning knives and the axe, and went down to work on the dead animal. Steve acted as though he was in a hurry to get down there, as if he had to prove to himself, quick like, that he hadn't missed. Such a serious error could weigh on a man's mind for a good long while. Sometimes a miss is the difference between life and death and it is not taken lightly.

When Steve got to the snow mound, he brushed the snow off to make sure there was in fact a buffalo there. Satisfied it was his buffalo, he felt redeemed.

"Even if I hada missed, nobody coulda blamed me. They wuz runnin and I couldn't see enuff ta git a good sight on 'em. Most anybody else wooda missed clean!"

"Yeah, I guess I gotta admit, that was a fair, good shot," agreed Shane.

"Whadya mean a fair, good shot! Why, that thar shot was a hunderd ta one, if I says so myself, which I do!" shouted Steve. "He didn't stagger more en a hunderd yards afore he keeled over! Fair, good shot my foot! It was a dang wondrous shot and ya knowed it, you young whippersnapper! I owe ya one!"

At that, Shane doubled over with laughter, slipped, and fell backward into a pile of bloody snow. H came up covered in the red and white mess.

This time it was Steve's turn to get the last laugh. Pretty soon both took to laughing because Steve had kept mumbling under his beard about what some people thought and what some people should keep ta their selves or some people wuz gonna get it! Shane's sides hurt, he laughed so hard.

Finally, Steve said, "We best get to work on this critter, as big as he is, it'll take us a couple days to get 'im all cut up. We'll need two horses ta hang 'im; he's bigger 'n two elk!"

With that, Shane went to the barn and got a rope. He threw a loop around one hind leg, pulling it tight to lift the leg, and tied the other end to a quakie. Steve began the big job of field dressing the bull.

Shane rounded up his mare and the paint and saddled both of them. This bull was half again as big as either of the horses. Probably weighed more than a ton with the guts in. Steve worked on the animal until he was knee deep in buffalo guts, with half of them still to go.

"Throw a rope around his head and drag 'im away from these guts so I ain't steppin' all over 'em tryin' to git the rest of 'em out," said Steve.

Shane untied the rope from the tree and the hind leg, then wrapped it around the head. He mounted his mare and looped the other end around the saddle horn and began to pull.

Lady could not get enough traction to drag the bull. Steve washed the blood from his hands in the snow, took a rope from his saddle, and put it around the bull's head as well. He mounted up, looped the rope around the horn, and they both pulled. The bull moved this time so they dragged it a short distance away.

"Fur enuff," said Steve, and he dismounted, untied his rope and continued the job. When Steve finished, they dragged the bull over to the Ponderosa pine between the shed and the barn.

Steve dismounted, unhooked the ropes from the animal, threw them over two different branches on opposite sides of the tree and tied one rope to each hind leg. He went to the shed and returned with two shorter pieces of rope. Climbing up the tree to the branches the ropes were on, he told Shane to pull with the horses. Shane took the reins on the paint, with both horses pulling, the buffalo slowly lifted off the ground. When the neck of the dead animal was just barely touching the ground, Steve tied his two short pieces of rope, one to each branch and then to each hind leg.

"Back up," he shouted to Shane. When the ropes had sufficient slack, he untied them and threw them to the ground. Shane collected up both ropes and tied them back to the saddles. He dismounted, loosening the girth straps of both horses, then pulled his knife from its sheath, to help with the skinning.

It took both men working nonstop the rest of that day to get the huge animal skinned and cut into pieces small enough for them to handle.

Each hindquarter weighed more than a man could lift and had to be cut into four pieces. Each backstrap provided fifty pounds of meat apiece.

By the time the sun was going down, Steve had removed the brain, wrapped it in the hide and stored it in the shed. It was completely dark and turning bitter cold by the time they had all the meat in the shed and the horses put up in the barn. This time Steve had removed one of the intestines from the animal and cleaned it. He would use this to make sausage from the heart and liver. He took this and one backstrap to the cabin with them. The cabin was cold, not having had a fire in it all day and the men were tired and hungry.

Shane started a fire in the cook stove. Steve took the backstrap and the intestine into the cellar and returned with some elk steak. Soon the cabin began to warm up. Steve put the cast iron skillet on the stove. Biscuits from breakfast were put in the oven to warm and elk steaks went into the skillet to cook.

Shane poured a cup of coffee for each of them and they sat down for the first time since early this morning. In a few minutes supper was ready and they began to fill their empty bellies. There was little conversation after dinner, as both men wanted nothing more than to crawl into their beds and sleep.

It took all of the next day to get the meat taken care of. Steve made a mixture of heart, liver, steak, dried chilies and wild sage that Shane had brought. He added salt and pepper to the mixture to make a sausage, and then stuffed it tightly into the intestine he had saved and hung it in the cellar to cure. With the elk, they now had over a thousand pounds of fresh meat to see them through the winter months. With an occasional rabbit or grouse, they would live like kings this winter. They spent the third day tanning the thick heavy buffalo hide. Those three days the sky was clear, the weather mild with most of the snow in the park melted.

Chapter 19

Indians

Early one morning in the spring, Steve awoke to find a small band of Indians in the park in front of the cabin. He recognized Ouray, Chief of the Utes, and some of the elders of the tribe. One appeared to be sick as he was lying on a travois.

Steve went out and was greeted warmly by Ouray, "It is good to see you again, Tevvy-oats-at-an-tuggy-bone (Big Friend).

"Greeting to the great Chief of the Ute, and The People whose land you have let me live on."

The sick one was another of the tribe's elders named Shavano and Steve recognized him when he got up close. Seems the sick brave had taken a lance from a Shoshone raid and all their Indian magic had failed to cure him. Ouray had brought him to Steve in hopes he had knowledge of white man medicine sufficient to make his sub-chief well.

Steve had been friends with the Ute for many years and had lived with them when he was younger. Steve agreed to take the sick brave and try to nurse him back to health. Ouray said he would be back in ten sleeps to either take his chief back with him or send him to the spirit world. With that, Chief Ouray and his band left the park, following the path the buffalo made earlier, leaving a horse and travois behind.

Shavano was very ill, running a high fever. He was close to death and barely conscious when they carried him into the cabin. Shane had a good knowledge of veterinarian medicine and some of this was common to humans as well. In fact, he had learned it was common to all living things. He had with him some medicine and mindful of the serious condition, began to tend to Shavano immediately. He compounded a mixture of natural herbs to treat fever and pain, which he had the patient drink along with some warm elk broth to give him strength. The wound, badly infected, was cleansed thoroughly before being stitched up. As Shane treated the wound, the young chief lapsed in and out of consciousness, which was good, because of the pain. When the wound was closed, Shane applied salve and clean bandages.

Just before dark, the patient awoke briefly, and Shane gave him more fever and pain medicine mixed with broth.

Shane stayed by the Indian's side throughout the night. Once more before dawn, Shavano awoke again to receive more medicine and broth.

During the night, Shane prayed that God would heal this man and bring him to a saving knowledge of Jesus Christ. By the middle of the next day, the fever had broken and the Ute took on a healthier color. The medicine and care were beginning to take effect. For two days Shane watched his charge carefully, nursing him slowly back to health. By the third day, his eyes were open; he was coherent and beginning to feel hunger. Shane kept the wound clean with fresh salve and it was healing nicely. The Indian began to take some meat with the broth so Shane knew he would survive. For the next two days, Shane watched the wound heal and the brave get stronger and stronger until he was able to sit up.

The sixth day the Indian could stand by himself and Shane knew he had proved himself as a medicine man with God's help. The next three days the brave spent getting his strength back. During this time, Shavano and Shane formed a bond of friendship that would last a lifetime. Each wanted to tell and show the other what they knew about everything. They were like two kids, each with a new toy to brag about.

As promised, after ten days, Chief Ouray returned. When he saw his chief was almost back to normal he whooped for joy and offered great thanks to Steve for saving Shavano's life.

"Wuzn't me done that Chief, my friend, Shane McQuaid, here done all the doctorin."

The old Chief went to Shane and said that anything he owned was now his. He took a necklace from around his neck and placed it around Shane's neck. The Chief said he would always be welcome in his lodge and whenever he came, there would be a great celebration and he would be given a place of honor among his tribe. He gave him the Indian name of Ahu-u-tu-pu-wit; Man-with-big-medicine.

After a ceremony of great thanks to Shane and the Great Spirit, the Indians mounted their ponies and rode out of the park.

When they reached the top of the ridge above the cabin, the Chief turned around and held his hand high in the air one more time to the man who saved his young chief's life. Shavano did the same.

"Looks like ya made a hit with 'em," said Steve as the old Chief disappeared into the timber.

"Yeah, reckon I did at that, to God be all the praise," answered Shane. "Never saw a person more appreciative. Gotta' remember to ride over and see him next summer. Maybe take him a gift or somethin'."

Steve chuckled, "Better be careful, you'll wind up marryin' one o' his daughters," cautioned Steve.

"How's that," Shane asked.

"Well, you give a gift to the Chief and he'll feel obliged to return the favor, and since you are such an important guest, it will have to be something special, like a bride or horse. Personally, I'd take tha horse!"

"I could probly do worse," laughed Shane. "At least I'd have someone who loved the wilderness as much as I do. She'd look out over this land and see what's really there. She'd be strong and could take care of herself. If I married one 'o those fancy ladies back East, I'd be forever havin' to take her back to see her mother. Wouldn't have no peace at all. That's sayin' she'd even let me come back here in the first place. Naw, I could sure do a lot worse than marryin' one of his daughters. Think I'll ride over next summer and check out the prospects!"

Steve raised an eyebrow and stared in disbelief at Shane. Somehow, he could not picture him married. Course he could be just joking, too. Besides, some of those 'prospects' might not be to Shane's likin. Steve figured it was a good time to change the subject. "Let's go drag them guts down the hill away from the barn. If it gits much warmer we'll have ever varmint in the country fer company."

They walked to the barn and saddled the paint and Lady. The two piles of frozen guts were solid and easy to tie a rope on. They dragged them down the hill toward the creek away from the barn, but within site of the porch so they could watch whatever critters came in to dine at Englert's Wild Gourmet Cafe!

They wanted them far enough away from the barn so the meat eaters wouldn't bother the horses but otherwise they enjoyed watching the many different animals that came to feed on the leftovers. Steve got a kick out of Shane naming a pile of guts after him.

From time to time, there would be coyote, badger, fox, wolverine, bobcat, eagle, and the ever-present raven and magpie. Only once did they see a mountain lion at the gut pile, but it stayed only a short while. Seems it favored the taste of fresh killed meat. They heard wolves there one night but never saw them. They spent much time on the porch watching the different animals come to feed. Nothing went to waste up here; every scrap was used. Some animals showed up for breakfast, others for supper, and the birds were there all day long. A wolverine might show up and run everything else off. They were so mean Shane wondered how they even got along with themselves. They fought with anything, regardless of size, even other wolverines.

"How do they make little wolverines?" Shane asked one afternoon.

"They don't," answered Steve. "They're born of fire and wind and ragin tornadoes. Then they're sent to hell fer an education. Trouble is they don't git along with nuthin down there neither and purty soon they gits kicked out and sent back up here."

That sounded like one wild fairy tale to Shane, but made it easier to understand their behavior. Steve said that story was told to him many years ago by a Wind River Shoshone medicine man.

Much of Steve's perspective on life was governed by Indian lore and legend. Much of it considered irrelevant by the white man, but it fit with the way he lived and he saw no reason to dispute most of the things the Red Man taught him. He had known many Indians and found them to be highly intelligent and honorable. He enjoyed the time he spent with them and agreed with their philosophy on life. He violently disagreed with the way the white man had exploited and cheated the Indian. and it was the primary reason he lived way up here. He welcomed any Indian into his company and in turn was highly respected and trusted by the Ute, Cheyenne, Sioux, Arikara, Blackfoot, Flathead, and even the Comanche and Apache, who fought terrible battles with the white man. One winter he spent time with the Mimbreno Apache, in Mexico, with their Chief Mangas Coloradas. There he became friends with a very tough Indian named Goyathlay. One day the Mimbreno invaded the town of Arizpe, and fought a two-day battle with Mexican forces. The second day of battle became a hand-to-hand melee where Goyathlay raged all over the battlefield. From that day on, this tough Indian became known as Geronimo.

Chapter 20

Jim Bridger - Mountain Man

One morning several days later, Steve and Shane were cutting firewood when a lone rider came into the park and rode toward the cabin. As soon as Steve saw him, he recognized Jim Bridger, a well-known fur trapper, trader and U.S. Army scout Steve had met years earlier at Bent's Fort down on the Picketwire. Having similar desires, they hit it off and became close friends. His given name was James Felix Bridger, but some of his friends called him Ol' Gabe. Jim rode up to the porch, his body leaning over the saddle horn, keen and wild eyes peering out from under the brim of his black and weathered hat.

"How ye be Englert?" Bridger inquired as he dismounted.

"Got nuthin' ta complain about Felix," Steve said as they shook hands and slapped shoulders. Steve introduced Jim to Shane and he shook his hand as well.

"Glad ta' make yer' acquaintance," he said in a low gravelly voice that sounded like a washtub full of rocks. Jim was a wiry man with gray hair; tough as an old boot. Shane had heard of some of his exploits and was amazed Steve and Jim were friends

Shane had read incredible stories of Jim while attending school back East and here he was talking to him. He remembered how he had felt when reading stories about this rough and tough fur trapper and his fighting, drinking and legendary knowledge of trapping.

During his time at school, Shane longed to be back in the mountains and hoped one day to run across this colorful figure and now he had just ridden right into their camp. This was a great day as far as Shane was concerned. Here was a giant of a man with a reputation rivaling that of Steve's. Here was a man who would surely be in the history books one day. Heck, he was there now. He sure was in the 'Dime Novels'!

"Come in and set a spell," said Steve. "I'll cook us up some elk meat and make some biscuits. Hope you'll be staying the night."

"Wouldn't miss yer cookin' fer nuthin," drawled Jim. "Much obliged fer the invite. Ya got any hot coffee?"

"Pot's always hot here. Come on in."

"I'll take care of yer saddle, sir. You best go on in and make sure Steve don't burn the coffee!"

"There he goes again, tryin ta give orders and tell me how to make coffee. Look Bub, I been makin coffee since afore ya wuz born!"

"Yeah, and it's a wonder nobody's died from drinkin it yet either!"

Jim just stood there not knowin what to think, until Shane winked at him. At which point he burst out laughing and gave Shane a slap on the back that would have knocked a smaller man flat on his face.

"Feels good in here," said Jim. "Ain't had a roof over my head fer moons. Been trappin' over on the South Platte till a freak snowstorm run me out. Snow up to the saddle horn down that canyon. Slept three nights in a snow bank till I cud wade outta there. Nearly lost the ponies, had to cut bark offa quakies to feed 'em. Cached the furs, they'll hafta wait'll later fer me ta git back in thar. Saw Ouray and some of his braves awhile back, aheadin' this a way. Had a travois, was too fer away ta see what they was a draggin."

Steve handed Jim a cup of coffee. "Shavano," said Steve. "Took a lance from a Shoshone. He brung 'em here and Shane patched him up."

"You a doctor?" asked Jim in disbelief, his eyes wide with surprise. Don't look like no doctor I ever seen afore."

"A horse doctor," answered Shane. "There's not much difference between a horse and a man when it comes to doctorin'."

"Well now, that's a first. Never been compeered to a horse afore. Smelt like one a few times tho," Bill laughed as he took a sip of Steve's coffee. "WAUGH!, how long you had this pot on? You could float a horseshoe on it! Jest like I like it," Jim said, as he winked at Shane.

"So yer a college man then?" asked Jim.

"Yes sir. Spent three long years in Boston learnin how to be a horse doctor."

"Don't see too many college edjacated folks up here. Too puny to put up with all the hardships I figgered. Never saw much use fer me ta git a edjacashun, formal like. A man gits lotsa learnin' just by bein' out here all tha time. It's mosly 'bout just how ta survive, which ain't too easy sometimes."

"It was hard fer me to live in Boston," continued Shane. "Too many folks back east, three years with no time off wuz all I could take. Was glad to be shut o' that place. Don't ever wanna go back. Course, there wuz one thing I took a fancy to...."

"What wuz that", Jim asked.

"Indoor plumbin'! Sure beats freezing yer backside and worryin' if you wuz gonna git stuck ta' tha' seat er sumthin' was gonna' come up and bite ya on yer you know what!"

Jim leaned his head back and roared. He laughed so hard tears came to his eyes. He leaned over and gave Shane another slap on the back.

"Steve, this here college man I like, he's all right. Where'd ya dig this youngin up"?

"I don't ritely knowed. He jest showed up one day and I kin't get rid o' him! Kinda like a wood tick that gits caught in yer whiskers!"

They all had a good laugh at that one, and then things settled down for a while.

The three men ate a hearty supper of elk, biscuits and coffee, and then sat around the stove talking afterwards. Steve filled his pipe and Jim put a wad of chewin' tobacco in his cheek.

"Passed thru Salida late last summer," said Jim. "Heard stories 'bout some fast horse that outruns thoroughbreds. Not just outrun 'em but run plumb outta site of 'em. The way they was a talkin, this horse sure was sumthin. Had them folks all stirred up. Heard one o' them fancy dans offered to buy that critter fer a hunderd thousand dollars. Never heard such a story afore. Must be some truth to it tho, the way they wuz all a carryin' on. Shor would like to see a horse like that jest once, afore my bones turn ta dust."

"That could be arranged," offered Shane. "I was the rider of that wonder horse. Everything they said is true. Fastest horse I ever seen. Out ran antelope with 'er one time. After I finished the race, I waited in town for a long time before the next rider showed up. Woulda had time to take a bath, get a shave, have a drink and go upstairs to check out the scenery, if I had wanted to, which I didn't. They wuz all ready ta lynch me before all the riders got in. They figgered I musta taken a short cut to get that far ahead. Didn't have ta cheat tho. I went by each marker fair and square. All the observers came in after the race and vouched fer me. When they realized I had won fair and square they all wuz wantin' to be my friend. One feller did offer me a hundred thousand dollars for my horse. Course, there wuz a couple of fella's that wanted something they couldn't have. I had to teach 'em a lesson, one, more than the other."

"Why? They try ta dry gulch ya?"

"Yeah, but I hope they learned their lesson and will think twice about tryin to steal a man's horse."

"What'd they look like?"

"Well, one fella was stocky built, about five foot seven with a knife scar across his nose and right cheek. The other was tall, maybe six foot, lanky build, with a mean lookin' face."

"Did the tall one have half of his right ear missin?"

"Yeah, that wuz an 'attitude adjustment' I gave 'im" Shane said.

"Well, I ain't sure what that thar attitudie adjustin' thing is, but I knowed them two. I think they work fer a dude up in Denver. No sorrier cusses ever walked tha earth. You best be careful with them two. They is bad medicine."

"Thanks fer the tip," Shane said.

"Where is this horse now," inquired Jim, his eyes wide with excitement.

"She's out in the park keepin' yer horse company," answered Shane.

Jim stood immediately and said, "Let's go take us a look see at this cayuse."

He was hardly able to contain his excitement. The three stepped out onto the porch and Jim pointed his finger toward the four horses grazing in the park.

"Must be her thar," he said spitting a big brown spot onto the ground.

Shane whistled and she trotted effortlessly up to the porch.

"Got markings like I ain't never seen afore, color's different to, looks like a cross 'tween a horse and tha wind. Strange, in a way, I can't put my finger on it, but she's all horse that's fer sure."

Shane gave Lady a biscuit and whispered something in her ear. She pretended to walk off but as she passed behind Bill, she reached down and snatched his gloves out of his back pocket.

"Hay, Whut the sam hill happened?"

Jim spun around and saw Lady looking at him with his gloves in her mouth.

.

"Gimme Back My Gloves!" Jim shouted as he made a grab for them. Quick as a flash, Lady jerked her head out of his reach. Bill tried again and again, each time unable to retrieve his gloves. "I give up. Make yer dang horse gimme my gloves back."

"Jim, just ask her nice," Shane said.

"What, ya want me ta talk ta yer horse?"

"Try it and see, Shane laughed."

"Ok. Lady, would ya mind givin' my gloves back?" Lady shook her head.

"Now What?"

"You forgot to say, Please."

Jim shook his head and turned to look at Lady, "Lady, give me my gloves, Please."

With that, Lady presented him his gloves, which Jim carefully took.

"If'n I hadn't seen it wit my own eyes, I'd never believed it." Jim said in amazement.

Shane asked Lady how old she was, Lady shook her head. He asked again.

Same response. "Oh, I git it, a lady never tells her age does she?"

Lady nodded her head, which brought laughs from Steve and Jim.

Shane patted Lady's neck, "You're a good girl, give Jim a kiss then go play."

Lady went to Jim, put her muzzle next to his whiskered left cheek, wiggled her upper lip then 'pranced' back to the others and continued grazing.

"Well, sit on a skunk! I never been kissed by a horse afore, a few ladies that looked like one tho."

That brought a round of laughter.

"I'd let you ride her but she just don't hanker ta anyone else on her back except me."

"That's Ok, I'm too old ta learn how ta fly anyhow," laughed Jim.

The sun was low on the horizon and streaked the evening sky with fingers of dazzling orange rays. Shadows crept up to the porch and the air took on a sudden chill.

"Best be puttin' the horses up fer the evenin'," said Steve.

The three walked to the barn, Shane got a bucket of oats, held it up and whistled. The four horses came on a dead run with Shane's mare arriving first by at least half the distance. They got them into the barn, fed them, shut the door and walked back to the cabin in the dark. Steve lit the lantern hanging it from a rafter. He filled his pipe with fresh tobacco then they all sat down with a cup of coffee and began to talk.

Actually, Steve and Jim did most of the talking; Shane was spellbound by the conversation. He was in awe of the stories they told, of the places they'd been, and the things they'd done and seen. They had many things to reminisce about. They told about being in Mexico, chased by an army of Federalis, and fighting with Mangas Coloradas on the side of the Apaches, and Pete Kitchen and how the Apache gave him a wide berth.

"One tuff hombre, that Kitchen fella," said Jim. They talked of fighting, trapping, and running all over God's Creation with only their curiosity to guide 'em, the dark of night to stop 'em, and sometimes not even that. They rode from sun up to sun down trying to get to the next horizon for no other reason than to see what lay beyond. The more they saw the more they wanted to see of this infinite wilderness. Over every hill were things more unbelievable than the last, breathtaking to the point a fellow had to stop, just to let his mind take it all in.

They talked of things so grand and unbelievable Shane could not imagine how a man could do so many things and cover so much ground in a lifetime. They spoke of the unimaginable jagged rocks in Wyoming Territory dubbed "Trois Tetons" by a Frenchman they ran across up there. They mentioned places and people Shane had read about in books.

All the places they had been to, and people they had personally known, who were already in the history books. Men whom Shane had read about and wondered in disbelief at their incredible exploits. Men who were giants in Shane's eyes and here he was sitting with two of the biggest giants of them all, listening to them tell tales of all the other giants.

They also talked of the fact that, as Jim was want to say "any human bein with half a brain knowed that all this wonder and beauty jest didn't happen by its self."

With that, Steve jumped in and said he didn't have much use for white man's religion. He knew that there had to be a supreme being that planned all things out and watched over it with a jealously that was to be respected and not taken for granted.

"You know Jim, Shane here has caused me ta do a good bit o' thinkin' bout the Great Spirit or as the kid says, God Almighty. For a guy that got his self all crammed full o' book learnin' and all that there other stuff, he's still got good sense, 'specially when he quotes stuff from the Bible."

"What stuff," Jim asked Shane.

"Well, do you fellers realize you both said just what God said in His Word? Steve and I have talked about a lot of things, but Jim, you really hit tha nail on the head when you said, 'anyone with half a brain knowed all we see didn't just happen by itself.' Steve, you related how you know there had to be a supreme being that created all this beauty. Well, that is just what the good book says."

Both men looked at each other in amazement, rather pleased with themselves, then looked back at Shane, wondering what he would say next.

"Fellas, you both are right in what you believe and ya know what? Ya know what ya believe, because God Almighty put that knowin' there Himself. It says that in the Old Testament, that God has set the knowledge of creation and eternity in the hearts of men. It also says it in the New Testament in the book of Romans. It is exactly what ya both just said. Do ya want to hear what the fellow that wrote most of the New Testament said?"

"Sure!" they both said in unison.

Shane got his Bible and opened it to Romans 1:18. "I'll read it kinda like we talk for the benefit of Steve here. He gits messed up on some o' these big words."

"Ya got that right," Steve laughed, He knew Shane meant no disrespect, but was just teasing, and also that Jim could barely read or write.

"Well, in the Book of Romans, it says that God's anger is against all those who knowingly lie and say what is not true. It says that what is true about God and what He created is known deep down inside of them. It goes on to say God put the truth of right and wrong in each man. It also says, that from the beginnin' of this world, God, His power and His nature have been understood through what was already made.

"Hay, that's jest what we said weren't it Steve", Jim replied, happy with himself.

"That's right, Jim, but listen to this last part. It says that some, even when they know the truth about God, they don't honor Him as God or give any thanks to Him, but just go their own way o' doin things.

"Ya mean there's folks that see all this wonder and beauty, and don't care how it got here or who done it. I knowed there is a lot that don't take care o' this land like the Indians do, but not wonderin who made it all is jest PLUMB LOCO!" Steve said.

"That's right Steve. It says those folks got all puffed up and thought they had everything figgered out. In fact, because they forgot about the

One that created them, their hearts and minds were messed up. They actually became fools and started makin all those figures, statues and stuff that looked like birds, animals and other things."

"Now that shore don't make no sense," Jim said.

"That's right, but get this, they also started talkin to em and worshipin them as if they had some magical powers!"

"Ya mean to tell me them folks carved up some animal out o' block o' wood and then started talkin' to it and askin' it fer help?"

"You got it, Jim."

"Shoot! Them folks is crazy as a loon!"

Just then, Steve spoke up, asking if they could pray for some of his friends that believed in that sort of thing.

"Sure Steve, that's a good idea. Who wants to start off?" There was silence from the two mountain men.

"How's bout ya startin off and we kin jump in later," Steve said.

"OK," Shane said. "Heavenly Father, we come to you with praise for who you are. We're askin for help concerning Steve's friends that don't really know you or your Son, Jesus. Open their eyes and hearts to see the truth of Your greatness and majesty as the Creator of the Universe. We ask that they all come to a saving knowledge that Jesus Christ is who He says He is and the only way for salvation and eternal life in heaven."

Just then Steve jumped in, "God, this here is me, I don't knowed as much as Shane here so forgive me if I don't git it all said right but I shore would prechate you helpin my friends understand who You is. That's all I got to say fer now, and I thank ya."

"I agree wit what he jest said!" Jim shouted.

"Heavenly Father, we ask all this in the name of Your Son, Jesus, Amen."

Just as Shane finished his prayer, using the name of Jesus and saying He was God's Son, Jim said, "I thought we wuz prayin' to God."

"Ah, Jim, you knot head, don't you knowed nuthin?" Steve said.

Jim turned and squared off at Steve, "Well, not much, but what I does knowed has kept me kickin longer 'en you, ya old buzzard!"

All of a sudden, silence! Then, both Jim and Steve broke out laughing, pounding each other on the back, as Shane let out the breath he just realized he had been holding. They laughed even harder as they looked at the shocked look on Shane's face.

"What's tha matter, Bub?" Steve asked.

"Not a bloomin' thing, now, but awhile ago I thought you two might come ta blows."

That brought even more laughter until finally Shane joined in. When everyone quieted down, Steve asked, "What wuz we talkin about?"

"Jim, you wanted to know who Jesus is," Shane said.

"Yeah, I'd like ta know more bout that feller too," said Steve.

"Jesus is the Son of God, plain and simple, no two ways about it! In the Book of John you will find more about who Jesus is than any other book in the New Testament. The New Testament is the group of letters that were written after Jesus went to be with His Father, God, in heaven. What you need to first understand is that the Holy Bible, is not only God's Word, it is His Words to ALL mankind. It was written by men, but what was written was under His direction. It records stuff about real people, real places and real events.

Those who believe, by faith, in who Jesus said He was, though they can't see Him right now, and ask Him to forgive them of the wrongs they have done and choose to make Him Lord of their lives, are called Christians. The Christian religion isn't based on myths or strange ideas that someone came up with. It's rooted and grounded in actual human history, of which you two are a part."

"You both have seen things that some would not believe and would call ya crazy! However, you both know they wuz true, you wuz there and saw it!"

"That's right," both said in unison.

"Well, most of the men who wrote the New Testament wuz there with Jesus also! They're livin proof of what occurred! "Jesus didn't just make the claim that He was the Son of God, He proved it many times and in different ways to thousands of folks."

"Jim, you'll like this one. Did ya know Jesus changed water into wine?"

"No kiddin, I knowed I wuz gonna like this here Jesus. What else did He do?"

"Well, He cured an important government official's son, He fed over five thousand folks with just a couple small fish and a loaf of bread, and He walked on water...

"Hold it right thar!" Jim said, "You say He walked on water?"

"That's right and He stopped the storm that was happenin at the same time!

He healed a man that was born blind and He brought back to life a friend who had been dead four days!"

"Now young feller, yer pullin' ma leg, I seen dead people afore and I ain't never knowed someone comin back ta life agin," Jim said.

"Me neither," said Steve.

"Me also, but think about this, if you are the Son of God, actually God in human form; I kinda like to say, God with skin on, nothin' is impossible. You created man why couldn't you raise him up good as new?"

Jesus was with God at the very beginning of creation. It says that Jesus is the spoken Word of God. He became a human and lived on this earth for a time, but He never ceased to be God. In other words, if you want to know more about who God is, look at Jesus. If you want to hear God, listen to His Son, Jesus"

"Jesus Himself said, "I am God's Son, if you have seen Me, you have seen my Father who's in heaven. Back in the days that He said that, He could have been taken out and stoned to death! He said a bunch of things that made the religious leaders of that day very mad. Eventually, they got one of his followers to betray him so that they could kill him.

"Hold on now, I thought ya said Jesus wuz God. How come he got kilt iffin he be God?" ask Jim.

"Yeah, that do sound kinda wrong, ya sure you got tha story right?" said Steve.

"Absolutely, you see, Jesus came to pay a debt owed that no one else could pay. The price paid was His willing sacrifice on a cross for us.

"Dang! I never heared o that kind o deal afore. That shur seems like a whole lot ta ask of someone." Jim said.

"Yes it was, Jim, but it had to be because of what Adam did, he was the first man that God created."

"What'd that skunk do ta cause Jesus ta have ta pay such a heavy price?"

"When God, with the help of Jesus, created earth, he created a very special garden called Eden. That's where he created and put Adam and his wife, Eve. God provided for their every need, they were in high cotton. They didn't even have to work. They had the run of the whole place, except one tree - the tree of the knowledge of good and evil. God said, "Don't eat its fruit."

"Nevertheless, they disobeyed and ate the fruit. As a result of their disobedience, they were kicked out of Eden."

"Hey, since God created them two, couldn't He seen to it that they couldn't eat that thar fruit you mentioned?"

"Yes, he could have Steve, but God didn't want puppets worshiping him. He wanted Adam and Eve to obey Him willingly. We are the only ones of His creation that God gave a free will. A will to choose for ourselves right from wrong, good or evil. Think about it. What would you want if you were God? A race of people who were made to worship You, or folks who would make a deliberate, free willed choice to worship You, love You, and fellowship with You?

"Ya got a point thar, Sonny," Steve said. "I shor wouldn't like folks tellin me they wuz my friend and inside they didn't like me, much less knowed me and what I wuz like."

"That's what tha Injuns call 'two faced, speaks with forked tongue,'" said Jim.

"That's right, Jim. Now, gittin back to Adam and Eve, they wuz tempted by Satan, I'll tell you about him later, because he wanted them to fail God's test of obedience. Sure nuf, they messed up; ate the forbidden fruit and BANG, sin, disobedience and death entered into the world. Remember what I told you about God, how He is Holy and therefore can't look upon sin? Well, when Adam and Eve sinned, that signed a death warrant for everybody that followed. You will have to agree, most folks are basically sinful. Big sin or little sin, bold face lie or little white lie, makes no difference to God. Sin is sin and it separates us from God just as it did Adam and Eve."

"Boy, that be a tough row to hoe!"

"Yes, it wuz. Now, here comes the good part. God promised that one day he would provide a way to restore mankind to a place of friendship, fellowship and eternal life with Him. That way is through Jesus. "That's why it says in tha Book of John, 'For God so loved the world that He gave His one and only Son, that whoever believes in Him (that's Jesus) shall not perish but have eternal life.' It also says no one gets to meet God except thru Jesus."

" Now hold on thar, what you mean thru Jesus"? Jim asked with a worried look.

"Patience, Jim, we're gonna git there. Now, in the Old Testament, that's the first half of the Bible, God set up a deal with His people. They could ask forgiveness and offer a perfect animal as a sacrifice for their sins and God would forgive em for one year. They had to renew this deal each year. Now, the problem was, the sins were not forgiven permanently, they were just pushed forward one more year! Only when God sent His Son Jesus, the perfect sinless offering, could sin be forgiven for all time. The price paid for all mankind was His death."

"Waugh! Hard ta believe anyone would give his life fer folks who ain't even been born yet." Bill said.

"Jim, you've heard about it. You know what 'Cut Covenant' is don't ya?

"Ya mean what Injuns do when they make ya a Blood Brother?"

"That's right. My life fer yer life if need be."

They spoke until daylight, at which time Jim stood, stretched his big frame and said, "Time ta head out. Much obliged fer the vittles and tha company."

Turning to Shane, he said, "Son I like ya. Ya speak truth and that's mighty hard ta come by some times. I'll think on all you've said."

" Jim, saddle yer horse and I'll have some grub and coffee goin when ya git back," Steve offered.

"Much obliged," Jim answered over his shoulder as he bent over and stepped through the door into the cold morning.

Steve had a hot breakfast ready when Jim got back with his horse. He let the reins drop to the ground and went back inside to fill his belly for the journey to Leadville. When they finished eating, Jim stood and offered his hand to Shane.

"Enjoyed yer company, hope our paths cross agin one day. Them wuz sound words and I'm thinkin I need to git more acquainted with that thar Jesus feller, might even go ta church sometime, if'n they'll let me in tha door." That brought a laugh from everybody because Bill most definitely did not look the church going type.

" Jim, if you see yer way to head to Salida instead of Leadville, you might wanna stop at that little church on the west side of town. Parson's name is Tim Swenson. He's a good man and I doubt he would care what you look like, even if you wuz draggin' a dead skunk with ya! He may need yer help. In fact, I think you could teach him a thing or two. It was a great pleasure to meet you and I enjoyed your visit more than anything else I can remember."

"Well I thank ya fer them kind words," he then turned and shook hands with Steve. "Much obliged fer the hospitality my friend. Can't say when I've had a better time or better grub. I'll be back thru here agin' one day." With those words, he mounted up and rode over the ridge, but not in the direction of Leadville.

"What an incredible human being," said Shane. "I heard tales of him back in Boston, can hardly believe he was actually here last night. Where'd you run across him?"

"Bent's Fort, 'bout thirty year ago. Four buffler hunters brave on whiskey jumped 'im one night. Cut 'im up purty good but afore he was done with them boys, two wuz kilt and the other two wuz beat plumb unconscious with broke bones and other things. He scalped one uv 'em and cut an ear off the other. I took him to ma tent and patched 'im up. Had ta stitch him up in several places. Been good friends ever since. A tougher man I never seen. Been all over hell and creation with Ol' Gabe."

"They talk of him back East almost like he ain't human, like he was someone who never lived, just dreamed up in somebody's imagination," said Shane.

"Ain't sure he's human, but he's dang sure real enuff," chuckled Steve.

Shane went to the barn to let the horses out to graze the park. Steve cleaned up the breakfast dishes and they spent the rest of the day doing chores around the cabin.

Steve put a pot of beans he had been soaking on to cook, thinking he would make beans and venison for supper. They cut firewood, patched a hole in the roof, fixed the steps on the porch, cut ice for the cellar and other chores that needed doing from time to time. Come sundown they put the horses in the barn and ate supper. They went to bed and slept like dead men.

Chapter 21

Big Paw

The next morning they awoke to find it had snowed a couple inches during the night. A brilliant deep blue sky greeted Steve as he stepped out onto the porch. He checked the gut pile but all he saw were the regular contingent of ravens and magpies. He stepped off the porch, walked around the corner of the cabin next to the woodpile, looking carefully for something as he walked. He soon found what he knew would be there—bear tracks. Came through last night just above the cabin, no more than a stone's throw away. The tracks were headed toward the top of the ridge, Steve walked back down the hill and into the cabin.

Shane was making coffee and Steve said, "Good day to go bear huntin'. We'll have us a cup and go find that critter."

"Did ya see him out there just now?" Shane queried.

"Saw his tracks on tha hill just above tha cabin; came thru last night."

"Wonder why he ain't hibernatin'," pondered Shane aloud. "Can't be nuthin' out there fer 'im to eat."

"Don't need nuthin' ta eat, today's his last day on earth," added Steve.

Shane cast a puzzled look toward Steve trying to figure out what he meant by that. "You sound like you expect that critter to just stand there and let you shoot him," said Shane.

Steve quickly replied, "Nope, I ain't gonna shoot 'im, I'm gonna' walk right up to 'im and stick 'im with my knife."

Shane's lower jaw dropped and he shook his head in disbelief. He thought Steve had lost his mind. "Never heard of a griz lettin' a man git close enough to poke a knife into 'im! Where in the world did ya get the all mighty idea ya could just waltz right up to a griz and stab him to death? Nobody in his right mind would ever think o' doin' that in his wildest nightmare! Tell me, did ya wake up this morning chewin on locoweed and find yer brains lyin' on the floor next to ya? I can't believe I'm hearin' what I'm hearin'!"

"Don't ya fret none," assured Steve." This here's all been planned out by someone higher 'n me. Pull yer boots on pilgrim and drink yer coffee. I'll go git the horses."

Steve went to the barn to saddle his paint. Shane showed up just as he threw the saddle over Lady.

"I hope ya know what yer doin'," he said.

Steve led the paint to the shed and went inside. He returned in a few moments with two ropes, his skinning knives and his axe. "Ya ready to go?"

"Ain't ya taking yer rifle?" Shane asked in absolute amazement when Steve climbed into the saddle without it.

"Don't need it, got muh knife," patting the large blade on his hip.

They rode up the hill to where they cut the bear's trail and followed the tracks into the timber. They were about a mile from the cabin when they caught up to the bear. He was in the trees next to a small clearing sitting on his haunches looking at the men as they approached.

They rode within a hundred yards and Steve dismounted. Shane tried desperately to think of something to say that would make Steve change his mind, but deep down he figured his friend knew what he was doing, at least he prayed he did.

"Hold muh horse," said Steve, "else he'll spook if the bear gits ta growling."

Shane held the reins as Steve approached the grizzly.

When he was within a few yards, the great bear stood to its full height. Shane shivered in the saddle as he saw the true enormity of the animal for the first time. It towered over Steve. Shane was beside himself with anxiety and fear. He thought to himself, if Steve doesn't have a trick up his sleeve or some powerful medicine on his side he's a goner for sure. He'd hardly make a good meal for that critter. He sat in the saddle, with his rifle cocked, in amazement, watching wide-eyed, his pulse racing.

Steve walked right up to the huge bear and without hesitating, plunged, using both hands, his knife, up to the hilt, into the bear's heart.

The animal made a roar that shook the heavens and made sounds that would scare rocks, then crumpled to the snow covered ground. The hair stood up on the back of Shane's neck and Steve's horse panicked. He had his hands full hanging on to his rifle, at the same time trying to keep the horse under control. Lady took it all in stride, which eventually seemed to calm the paint.

When he finally got the paint calmed down, he noticed Steve was motioning for him to come over. The horses would have none of that though, they smelled bear and blood and neither sets well with horses. He dismounted and walked over to where Steve stood over the gigantic bear.

Shane lifted a front paw and put it next to his own hand for comparison. His hand looked like the hand of a baby compared to a full-grown man next to the bear paw. The dark brown, ivory tipped claws were longer than his own fingers. He tried to lift the massive head but could only move it a little. He lifted the lip up to look at the teeth and found one fang missing. The other fang was almost as long as one of the claws.

Shane was shaken to the point he could hardly speak. His hands were trembling; beads of sweat were on his forehead. He was having trouble standing on his own, so he sat down on the bear to collect his senses. He could not force himself to believe what he had just seen. What power did Steve have at his will that would give him the strength to walk up to a full-grown griz and kill him single handedly with one thrust of a knife? There was something here that Shane could not understand. Completely overwhelmed; his mind racing, he became aware of a human voice talking to him as he felt a hand on his shoulder. When he got back to normal, he realized it was Steve.

"Thought I might lose ya thar fer a minute, pilgrim," he said. "Yer eyes wuz gittin' all glazed over and you wuz havin' a hard time breathing'. Ya gonna' be all right or am I gonna' hafta work on this critter all by myself.

Shane came back to the real world, stood up, and said, "Yeah, I'll be ok, was just havin' a hard time believing all this. Still don't know that I ain't dreamin."

"Well, we ain't sleepin so how could we be dreaming," quipped Steve. "Let's git this critter cleaned out and drag 'em back to the cabin. See if the horses' will come up here."

Shane walked back to fetch the horses. To his surprise, although a little hesitant, they followed him right up to the bear. They sniffed the carcass and once satisfied it was dead, calmed right down.

Steve took his knife and began the job of field dressing the huge animal. The work was harder and took a lot longer than an elk but not as long as a buffalo. When the guts were lying in a pile next to the bear, Steve looped both ropes around the animal's head and tied the other ends to a saddle horn each. They mounted up and began the trip back to the cabin. It was a quick journey as the huge bear dragged easily because of the snow, and presently they pulled up in front of the Ponderosa pine next to the shed.

Steve dismounted and went into the shed returning with his two short pieces of rope. Using the same method they employed to hang the buffalo, they soon had the griz suspended ready to be skinned. A bear is harder to skin than an elk or a deer; a grizzly even harder. The hair is long and thick and doesn't peel off as easy because of the shape of the carcass, which is more rounded than an elk.

The skin will actually tear if pulled on very hard. This was a monstrous animal; Steve figured it weighed close to thirteen hundred pounds alive. Hanging in the tree as it was, Steve couldn't reach the rear claws with his axe!

"Must be close to twelve feet long," he drawled.

Shane entered the shed and returned dragging a wooden table. He positioned it next to the bear, "We'll have to stand on this to reach his hind legs."

They worked carefully with the skinning being careful not to cut holes in the skin or tear it. It was late afternoon before they finished the tedious job. They stretched the hide out on the snow, marveling at the size of it. It was larger than any elk hide they had in the shed.

"Ain't hardly got a wall on the cabin big enough for this critter. Could put it on the roof and use it fer a blanket!" Steve laughed.

It was late that night before all the meat was off and they dragged the carcass down to the gut pile. They carried the table back into the shed and stacked the meat on it. This would be good eating in a few days after it cured a little.

Bear meat is a delicacy fit for a celebration and this was certainly cause for a celebration. It isn't everyday you kill the most dangerous and feared animal in the forest with a knife. They fried potatoes and elk meat in bear fat, made biscuits, and had a royal feast. They filled their bellies until they could hold no more then, bone tired, went to bed. You could hear their snoring clear to the creek!

That night Shane had a strange and wonderful dream. He saw himself sitting on a rock looking at a little creek with an abundance of wildflowers lining the banks. The atmosphere was peaceful, the soft breeze fragrant with the scent of wild strawberries and the sound of crystal clear water running over smooth polished river rocks. All of a sudden, he saw Lady raise her head and move closer. Then from somewhere within himself, he heard...

"My son, this is your Heavenly Father. I gave you wisdom and abilities while you were yet in your mother's womb. Remember my Son's story about the three servants and the money they were given. I expect you to use what you have been given wisely and not just for your own gain or benefit. You will begin to hear My voice more clearly as you are careful to listen. Test that which you are unsure of according to 1 John 4, "Did Jesus Christ come in the flesh?"

"My son, I am pleased with your love and awe of all I have created, be careful not to worship the created instead of the Creator. Just as I created the wonders of heaven and earth, I also created man to fellowship with Me. That is the reason I sent my Son; that man might have life eternally through Him. I will do great things through you if you have the courage. Ask of Me. Trust that My Word will not return to Me void but will accomplish where I send it and it shall prosper in doing so. Believe in My Word. It is the most powerful force in the universe. Act on it. I will guide you. We will speak more later. Yes, Jesus Christ, came in the flesh and is even now seated with Me in heaven. I Am that I Am and have spoken."

Early next morning Shane dressed, built a fire in the cook stove, put the coffee on and quietly slipped out the front door. Standing on the porch, he looked heavenward. "Father, I trust you with my life. Lead me as You will. I will serve you as best I can, but I will need your help. Thanks for lovin' me, Amen." With that, he went into the cabin to get a cup of coffee and start breakfast.

The weather was warm, the sky clear. There were many crows at the gut pile feasting on the carcass of the grizzly.

They nailed the bear hide onto the wall next to the woodpile. It nearly covered the entire wall. They now had few chores except to graze the horses and chop firewood. They appreciated the free time. Shane found this a good time to read his Bible and Steve always gave him space to do so. Every now and then, he would ask Shane a question and Shane would look it up and then they would discuss it.

One warm afternoon as they sat on the porch, Shane was looking at the pile of bones from the grizzly and said, "Steve, I never asked why ya kilt that bear the way ya did. I figgered ya had yer reasons and it weren't none o' my business. But if it ain't pryin' I sure would like to know."

"I don't mind tellin ya. In fact it wuz yer doin!"

"Mine?"

"Yep, ya told me I cud pray to God Almighty and He would hear and help me if'n I needed it.

So I did and He did and that's tha end o that."

"Now, hold on a minute, ya can't leave me hangin out like that. Ya mean God told ya to kill Big Paw with yer knife and tha bear would let ya?"

"Yep! He said that bear wuz old and tired o' livin, so He sent him ta me to give him a' honorable end. It wuzn't me done it on my own. Ya think I'm crazy? You said pray, listen fer His voice, be sure it's Him, then jest trust 'em to help. That's all I done. Did I git sumthin wrong?"

Shane shook his head in amazement, "No Steve, you got it just right."

The rest of that winter was relatively mild. It never got down to thirty below as it had in years past. There was a lot of snow but enough time elapsed between storms that most melted before it had a chance to accumulate. On the north, facing slopes, the snow layered in great depths but wherever the sun could reach, it melted exposing the buffalo grass and afforded grazing for elk, deer, bighorn and horses. The horses would graze right along with them and were accepted as their own kind.

One day late in the fall, Steve and Shane were watching a herd of Big Horn Sheep. Two of the large males were fighting it out by butting their heads together, producing a very loud crash as they connected.

Steve retorted, "I wonder if it gives them big woolies a headache when they do that?"

Shane laughed and instead of giving him the medical answer just said, "Naw, they just go eat some juniper berries and they're fine." He waited for what he knew was coming.

Several minutes later, "Juniper Berries! Whut's that gotta do with it?"

"Yer kiddin', I thought ya would know about Juniper Berries. Don't ya know that's whut they use ta flavor Gin, a type of booze they drink back East."

"Never heared uv it. Is it any good?"

"Well, that all depends on how sophisticated ya are."

"That leaves me out! I'll ask the bartender in Granite next time we're over that way. My, my, so that's what keeps them rams from gittin a headache. Ya think it'd work fer me?

"Don't know, ya might give it a try and let me know. Medical science would greatly appreciate any information you could give them."

Shane was having a very hard time keeping a straight face. Lord only knew what would happen if Steve did what he said, then found out he had been duped. Juniper berries weren't the most pleasant tasting things you could put in your mouth!

Early one morning in late spring, Shane built a fire in the cook stove to make coffee then stepped out on the porch to watch the sunrise. Shortly, Steve poked his head out.

"Mornin," he said as he stepped out and offered Shane a cup of coffee.

"How bout we git us some vittles and take a ride up to the top o' the range and look around today?"

"Sounds good ta me," Shane said.

The sun was up and melted the frost off the porch by the time they finished breakfast. Steve went to the barn to saddle the horses. By the time he had them both saddled, Shane had finished the dishes. Steve put his other horse out to graze while they were gone, knowing he wouldn't leave the park. They mounted and rode toward the sagebrush hill and to the top of the range.

Chapter 22

Grizzly!

"Race?" yelled Shane.

"Sure," yelled Steve. He was in the lead at the time, so he figured, with a head start, he had a chance. The race was immediately on and almost as quick Steve was in second place losing ground fast. Lady shot by him and flew up the hill, covering the mile to the top of the ridge in very little time. Shane went over the top and disappeared. Steve continued up through the sagebrush at a gallop. Just as Steve was about to reach the top he met Shane coming back over at full speed.

"GRIZ!" he yelled as he flew by and then the great bear was on top of Steve.

The bear stood on his hind legs and took a swipe with a giant paw raking his deadly claws across the flank of the paint. The horse reared sideways nearly dumping Steve in the process as horse and rider went down with the bear on top.

Shane stopped Lady when he saw what had happened, taking his Spencer from the scabbard, a look of horror on his face.

Steve had rolled free but the bear had his jaws locked on the saddle horn as the saddle had slipped almost underneath the horse. Horse and bear rolled down the hill. The paint made one last desperate attempt to escape. Frantically kicking and flailing it caught the bear square on the side of his head with a hind hoof, momentarily stunning the animal, causing it to let go of the saddle. The paint got to her feet and bolted, panic stricken, toward the cabin the stirrups dangling along the ground.

While the bear was trying to regain its senses, Shane began pumping bullets into the dazed animal. Steve stumbled towards Shane as the bear got to its feet and charged after him. Steve could not run very fast because his right leg had been injured when he fell. He hobbled down the hill as fast as he could as bullets flew over his head.

Steve could hear the bullets hit the animal causing the bear to roar with wounded fury as he charged down the hill. Steve tripped over a bush and rolled head over heels, feeling the hot breath of the bear on his neck. Turning, he drew his knife, thrusting it deep into the chest of the bear as he looked up into the gaping jaws of death, blood dripping from its mouth. He saw one of the giant fangs was missing and his last thought before he was knocked unconscious, "Was that Big Paw had come back to haunt him."

Steve thought he was dreaming, and he thought he heard voices. He opened his eyes to see Shane kneeling over him. A searing pain shot through his left shoulder and right leg. He looked down at his feet and saw the body of the bear lying across his legs. He tried to sit up but his shoulder hurt too badly. His legs felt like they were being crushed by the body of the bear.

"I can't move the bear," Shane hollered, "He's too big. I'll try to drag him off with my horse while you try to drag yourself out from underneath." Shane looped his rope around the massive head of the grizzly and mounted Lady. He managed to pull the animal over and Steve painfully rolled to one side. Shane left the rope on the animal, hurrying back to see if Steve was all right.

Steve could see a concerned look on Shane's face and immediately knew why. The ground was covered with blood where he had been laying. His shoulder was on fire and pain raged through his right leg. Shane helped him sit up, his shoulder dangled uselessly at his side. His elk skin coat had been ripped away with blood running down the torn sleeve. Shane removed the shredded material to more closely examine the wound. He retrieved a cloth from his saddlebag and brought his canteen to give Steve a drink.

He wiped the blood away and said, "Ain't as bad as I was spectin, but a good gash to be sure." He wrapped the wound and helped Steve to his feet. He couldn't put any weight on his right leg at all. Gotta' git ya back to the cabin and get that bleedin' stopped," Shane said worriedly. He removed the rope from the grizzly and helped Steve onto Lady.

Steve winced with pain as he swung his right leg over the back of the horse. He almost passed out, causing him to nearly fall off the other side. Shane had to hold onto him to keep him in the saddle. Steve gritted his teeth and hung onto the saddle horn with his right hand. He leaned forward into the saddle and hung on as best he could. Shane led Lady back to the cabin. Shane noticed that Lady took extra care as they walked back to the cabin. Shane situated Lady next to the porch as close as he could and eased Steve out of the saddle.

Shane helped Steve into the cabin, laying him down on the wide bench against the wall. Opening the door to the cook stove, he discovered red coals and threw in some more wood to heat water. He returned to Steve and removed the rest of his shirt and boot, which brought a cry of pain. The leg was already beginning to swell but did not appear to be broken. Shane returned his attention to the bloody shoulder.

"Bleedin's almost stopped," he said. "That's a good sign, means it ain't too deep. He rinsed out the bloody cloth with warm water, washing the wound, and exposed three cuts along the back of the arm.

"Looks like he missed ya with a couple of his claws. Good thing, probably would have taken yer whole shoulder off. Cuts ain't too deep. Yer shoulder I spect is dislocated by the look of it. Hang on and I'll put it back in place." Shane got up, went to a kitchen cabinet and got a bottle of whiskey. "Here, take a few slugs of this, yer gonna need it." Steve did as he was told then laid back on the bench with his eyes closed.

With that, Shane drug a chair over, sat down and took his right boot off. He gently raised Steve's left arm straight out, which brought a yelp of pain. "Sorry, buddy." He then placed his sock coated foot in Steve's armpit and before he could offer any objections, Shane snapped it back into the socket as Steve let out a yell and passed out. Later, after a massage and herb tea, laced with whiskey, the pain in his shoulder, except for the cuts, was much better. Shane finished cleaning them out, covered them with salve, and a bandage. (Steve would later tell folks how Shane had tried to pull his arm off, but couldn't.)

"Don't know that I can do much fer yer leg," Shane said. Looks like yer horse rolled on it. It's gonna be real sore fer awhile, but I spect you'll be back to normal in a couple weeks. Best go see if I can find the paint. The way she lit out, could be in Leadville by now."

Shane left Steve lying on the bench, went outside, and mounted his mare. Just as he was about to ride away he saw the paint coming toward the cabin about a quarter mile away. He rode over, noticing its left flank was covered with blood. He dismounted to take a closer look. There were four deep gashes about a foot long on the left rear flank of the horse.

"Well, looks like yer gonna' need some stitches to fix those up," he said to the horse.

He took her reins, mounted Lady, and led the wounded horse back to the barn. Inside, he hobbled and tied the paint so it couldn't move while he stitched her up. He walked to the cabin where he found Steve sitting at the table drinking a cup of whiskey laced coffee.

"Cept fer ma leg, I feel purty good. Did ya find ma horse?"

"Yep, needs some stitches though. That griz gave her a good swipe on her left flank. Came to get the salve and my bag. Don't worry, she'll be fine." Shane said over his shoulder as he went out the door with bag in hand.

Looking through his bag, Shane found no thread to sew up the paint. A few strands of the horse's tail would work just as well. He cleaned the cuts out thoroughly and with needle and thread made of horsetail, he sewed up the four gashes on the horse's flank, and covered his handiwork with salve. After untying the horse, he led her back out to the park and went to the house to check on Steve. He found him gingerly trying to put weight on his right leg and wasn't having much luck. Shane shook his head, "You are one stubborn ol' coot!"

"Well, I might be that, but I'm a live one thanks ta you. Pour yerself a cup, sit down and tell me what the samhill happened this mornin,"

Shane got his coffee then gave the following account. "I rode over the top of the ridge and was nearly on top of the griz before I seen 'im. Musta heard me comin' and hid, tryin' fer a ambush, but I saw him just in time as he rose up. I had time to turn and head back over the hill, where I seen you comin' up the hill.

The griz was hot on my tail but Lady out ran 'im. By the time I got stopped and turned around, I seen the bear knock you and yer horse to the ground. The bear and the horse went rollin' down the hill. I took my rifle out ready to start shootin' and yer horse kicked the bear in the head and got away. I commenced ta' shootin' at the bear and by now you wuz runnin' toward me with the bear hot on YER tail. I could see you wuzn't gonna' make it the way you wuz a cripplin' along. I knew you wuz a goner, when you fell, but I kept shootin' anyway. I was aiming' for his mouth, hopin' I could keep him from eatin' ya. Did shoot one of his teeth out, but I ran outta bullets!

By that time, you wuz on yer back with the bear standin' over ya ready to tear ya in two. I put two more bullets in and that's when you stabbed the critter with yer knife. I fired twice into his head and he just fell over. I loaded more bullets and dismounted. The bear wuz dead when I got there and I thought you wuz too. That's 'bout when you woke up. You know the story from there."

"When I looked up and saw that fang missin', I figgered that Big Paw had come back to haunt me. Figgered I wuz a goner this time. It's a good thing ya knowed how to shoot that rifle. Glad somebody 'vented one o' them things that shoots more'n once afore ya gotta' reload. I better git me one o' those. Dagnabit! Tha' bear population 'round here is gittin plumb intolerable. Gittin' ta where ya can't sling a dead skunk without hittin' a griz. Did ya see my Hawken layin' up there anywhere's?"

"I didn't even think about yer rifle. It wasn't on the horse when I found her. Probably fell outta the scabbard when y'all were rollin' 'round on the ground, playin' with that critter. Best go see if I can find it. Be right back."

Shane went out, found Lady still standing where he had dropped her reins. Mounting up, he lit out for the top of the ridge. He rode past the carcass of the bear and up the hill where the first encounter took place. There, among the broken landscape and trampled sagebrush was the Hawken. The stock was busted clean in two. Shane dismounted and picked up the broken firearm. The barrel was bent into a dogleg shape. He held it up and said out loud, "Bet ya could shoot around a corner with this." He mounted up and rode back to the bear. It was lying on its side just as they had left it earlier. He dismounted and began to kick around in the dirt looking for Steve's knife. All he found was the bone handle.

"Musta busted off when the bear fell on it," He thought.

At the time, Shane didn't feel like digging around inside the bear to retrieve the blade so he mounted up and rode back to the cabin.

Steve was sitting on the porch when he pulled up.

"Here's what's left of yer shooter," handing the damaged firearm to his friend.

"Yup, looks like a good excuse to git me another 'un. Dang! I could shoot a circle with this and hit myself in the back o' the head," he said, holding the bent rifle up as best he could with his good arm. "Soon as I git healed, up we'll head fer town and scare up one like yers."

Shane dismounted, took the saddle and blanket off the mare and let her graze. Putting the saddle on the porch, he sat down next to Steve who was inspecting the Hawken.

"Busted clean in two," he said. "Wonder how it got bent in a circle like that. Ain't no teeth marks on it; horse musta just rolled over the dang thing. Didn't happen to see my knife up there did ya?" Shane reached down inside his shirt and handed what was left of the knife to Steve.

"Just wurn't my day," Steve muttered. "Got that knife from Chief Joseph up in the Bitterroot country many summers ago it wuz. Gave it to me as a gift. Smart man that Injun; fought the Army to a standstill with mostly women and old men. Reckon he'll be in the history books one day. Interestin' story if they tell the truth about 'im. Him and his people are livin' in Washington territory now on a reservation."

Steve looked like he was in more pain than he was lettin' on, so Shane made him a drink with elk root for pain, "Drink this, along with the 'Oh Be Joyful' ya got in ya. It'll help what ails ya." Steve drank it but sure made a funny face as he did.

"God, that's awful! Ya tryin to kill me or just make me feel worse? Dang! Jest as soon chew on a cow patty as drink that stuff!" Shane just laughed.

Just after sundown, Shane put the horses up and fixed supper. He gave Steve more herb tea to ease the pain, which produced more grumblin' from the patient about how Shane was tryin to poison him. They went to bed early. It had been a trying day.

Before dawn, Shane was awakened by Steve rattling around in the kitchen trying to light the lantern one handed.

"Ya got sumthin' against sleep?" Shane inquired.

"Feels like ma laigs 'bout ta bust open," he answered in the dark.

"Better lemme take a look at it," said Shane as he got up and pulled on his breeches.

By now, Steve had the lantern lit. Shane had him sit down so he could inspect the painful appendage. It was horribly swollen and starting to turn the color of a plum just before picking time. Shane examined it closely; it felt hot to the touch so he knew there was some infection the body was trying to fight off. He was sure it was not broken, but it was swollen all the way up to the knee.

"You gotta badly bruised lower leg. That's the reason it's inflamed and swollen. That is also the reason for the pain. I'll give ya something to ease the pain, but since we have no snow for the swelling, yer gonna have ta tough it out. Probly been better off if you had broke it," he said. "Coulda just shot ya and put ya outta yer misery, then I could get a good night's sleep. This is gonna' pain ya fer quite a few days and look even worse, but at least it ain't gonna' kill ya. You'll just have ta cripple around on it till it gets better. I would suggest you stay off of it as much as possible, keep it elevated, which will help reduce the pain and throbbing. I would also like to pray for your leg, if it's ok with you?"

"Go right ahead, it can't hurt."

"No, but it might help the pain," Shane said.

"Heavenly Father, I lift up my friend, Steve, to ya and ask that You supernaturally heal his leg. Take the pain, swelling and inflammation away. I speak life and healing to every part of this injured leg. Leg, in the name of Jesus, be healed! Amen."

"Thanks, Son, shore prechate that."

You stay put, I'll make the coffee and fix breakfast. Shane stirred the coals in the cook stove, threw in some kindling and smaller pieces of wood. Presently, he had a good fire going and put a pot of coffee on.

"What do ya think we oughta do with that bear?" he asked Steve.

"Cut the claws off and leave the rest fer coyote bait," was his terse reply. "Got no use fer the hide since ya shot it full o'holes! By now, the meat ain't no dang good anyway. Do ya mind cuttin the head off and puttin it on the porch next ta the other one, that way we'll have a matchin' set!"

"OK," laughed Shane, "as soon as the sun comes up I'll go tend to it."

Shane's diagnosis concerning the length it would take Steve's leg to heal was wrong. Later in the day as he rode up to the cabin dragging the grizzly's huge head, he saw Steve standing on the porch.

"I thought I told you to keep off that leg!"

"Don't need ta, it don't hurt no more."

"What!" Shane swung down from his horse and told Steve to sit down. He then pulled up Steve's pant leg and was shocked to see a perfectly normal leg. No swelling, no discoloration. He squeezed it, "Feel any pain?"

"Nope."

"Praise God! Thank you Jesus! Pardner, yer healed by tha power of God!"

Shane was beside himself. He hugged Steve, hugged Lady, and hugged himself.

"Thank you, Lord, to You be all the glory! Please forgive my lack of faith."

He turned to Steve, "I want to hear all about it"

"Bout what?"

"About yer leg, dummy!"

"Which one?"

"Yer Right One!"

"OH, That One!"

"YEAH, That One!"

"Well, after you left, I got me a cup o' coffee and came out here to sit and prop ma' laig up like ya said. It wuz hurtin' somethin' awful. I thought if I'd look at sumthin else it'd take ma' mind off the pain.

Well, there wuz' somethin' goin on down at the bone pile so I wuz' thinkin' hard on that. All of a sudden, I noticed ma' laig weren't hurtin' no more. I pulled up ma paint leg and it looked normal! I just started shoutin' and thankin' God Almighty. I wuz' jumpin' and hoppin' around on that right leg and it didn't hurt none. And that wuz that!"

"Steve, I'm overjoyed. I know how much that leg must have hurt. WOW, Thank You, Jesus!"

"Amen to that!" Steve was quiet for a while then said, "Shane, I thinks I need ta git ta know this feller ya' call, Jesus, kin' ya' help me with that?"

"Steve, I would be proud to introduce you to my Lord and Savior, Jesus Christ. I sure know He wants to meet you! Let me get my Bible.

"Steve, Jesus said, 'the thief, that's Satan, comes only to steal, kill and destroy.' Jesus said, 'I have come that they, that's you and me, may have life, and have it to the full'. You remember me telling you that because the first man went and did what he wanted, not what God wanted, it resulted in separation between man and God.

"Yeah, that weren't no good!"

"Yer right Buddy, look here in the Book of Romans where it says that the wages of sin is death. There's that separation from God; but lookie here, it then says that God gave us the gift of eternal life through His Son, Jesus Christ. That means a believer will never die, but live forever with God and Jesus in heaven.

"Now that's what I calls a shor nuf good bargain. Go on, tell me some more."

"Well, all through history, man has tried ta bridge that gap between himself and God. He's tried good deeds, religion, philosophy, being an extra good person, and other crazy stuff and ya know what, none of it MATTERED A HILL OF BEANS!"

"How come?"

"There is only one remedy for the problem of sin and separation, that's Jesus Christ. When Jesus died on a cross and rose from the grave on the third day, He paid the penalty for our sins and bridged the gap between God and man. Look here in the fifth chapter of Romans. God demonstrates His own love for us in this: While we were still sinners, Christ died for us. It says here, in the first chapter of John, that to all who receive Him, that's Jesus; He gives the right to become sons of God. Jesus Himself said that He stands at the door to your heart and knocks, if any man hears His voice, and opens the door, He will come in to him."

"So yer sayin that there be only one way I kin git this here eternal life and that be by acceptin' God's Son, Jesus, and all He said bout Hisself?"

"That's right. It says that by God's grace, yer saved, through faith in Jesus. But get this, it goes on to say that God's grace, which means favor you didn't earn, is a free gift from Him and not sumthin you can do on your own. Steve, would you like to have Jesus be tha Lord and Savior of your life?"

There was silence in the cabin for several minutes. Then......

"Yeah, I would, but ya gotta help me with tha right words. I don't want ta make no mistake on this."

"Steve, just repeat after me, "Dear Lord Jesus, I know that I am a sinner and need Your forgiveness. I believe in my heart that You died for my sins. I ask Your forgiveness for the things I done wrong, wither I knew it or not. I invite You to come into my heart and life. I want to trust You as savior and follow You as Lord of my life. In Your name I pray, Amen."

Steve finished repeating what Shane had prayed, said "Amen," and then looked up. Shane could see wetness in Steve's eyes. There was a look on the old trapper's face Shane had never seen before. All of a sudden, Shane started praising God as tears ran down his own cheeks.

"Well, ya don't have ta git so emotional bout it young feller. Look what ya went an made me do," Steve said as he wiped his own wet eyes.

Both men looked at each other, and then broke out laughing, hugging each other and in general having a great time. Eventually, when things settled down, Steve said they needed to head to Granite for supplies and a new rifle.

"Well, yer paint needs a few more days to ensure her wounds are healed enough for the stitches to be removed. Give her about another week and we'll see how she's doing."

Steve looked disappointed at the news, then suddenly turned to Shane and asked, "Why don't we pray fer my horse and ask God Almighty to heal her up quick?"

Shane looked surprised, then laughed, "Well, I've never heard it put quite like that before, but I don't see any problem with it. He healed an ornery cuss like you, why not yer horse!"

"Who ya callin ornery? I ain't ornery, that's jest ma good nature showin' thru."

"Well, since yer so good natured, how about you prayin' fer yer horse."

"Me! I don't knowed how ta do that. Wats I suposed ta say?"

"Just talk to Him like ya talk to me, come on, you can do it. God doesn't care that ya murder the English language; He loves you and wants to hear from you in yer own words. I think He can make sense out of it."

"Well, OK, here goes... Hold it, which one does I pray ta, God Almighty, Jesus Christ or the one called Lord and Savior?"

"Well, which one do ya wanna talk to?"

"Well I guess I'll talk ta Jesus cuz he's tha one what saved me."

"Good choice, brother, I know He will be pleased to hear from you, regardless of how you pronounce yer words."

"Look Bub, I talks jest fine. Ain't nuthin wrong wit my speech and I didn't murder no dang English guy either!"

"OK, here goes, Lord Jesus, would You do me a favor an heal my ol' horse real quick, soze me and Shane kin go to Granite and git what we're a needin. I knowed you kin do it and I thank ya, if'n yer a mind ta doin it. Oh, agin' I thank ya fer savin' me, I'll never fer git ya fer that. Amen!"

"Well, don't jest stand thar, COME ON!"

"Come on where," asked Shane.

"Ta see Jesus heal my horse, ya dummy!" Steve yelled, as he trotted toward the barn.

Shane looked at Steve, who was already at the barn, and shook his head, "Lord, sure would appreciate help here," and trotted after him. He hadn't reached the barn when he heard Steve give a whoop and poke his head out the barn door.

"Come a runnin, pard, ya gotta see this, it's tha dangest thang I ever seen!"

As Shane rounded the corner, Steve was standing, wide eyed, next to his horse. What he saw next shook him to the very depths of his spiritual core.

As he watched, a wound that was made by four, 3½" long, grizzly bear claws was already almost totally healed. In less than five minutes, there were no signs that the paint had ever been hurt.

Steve was whoopin' and jumpin' around, huggin' his horse, and patting the place where the bear had wounded him. He was beside himself with joy and amazement.

"I told ya He could do it, didn't I? Thank ya, Lord Jesus, yer welcome in ma cabin anytime you want!"

Shane turned away, walked out of the barn, looked up and said, "Lord God, please forgive me again for my lack of faith. You have again shown Yourself powerful and merciful. Thank You for giving Steve child-like faith in You and Your Son. Please, give me a dose of that same faith; I sure need it, in Jesus name, Amen."

Chapter 23

Granite

Early the next morning they saddled up and rode for Granite. Most of the snow was gone now from the high country. Only on the dark timbered north facing ridges and above timberline in rock crevices was there any snow at all. The columbines were in bloom everywhere and the quaking aspen were beginning to show a light canopy of green all along the ridge south of the park. The beaver ponds up and down the creek were alive with feeding fish.

Summer would soon be in full swing. As they rode along the creek, Steve said, "'Bout time ta unlimber ma fly rod. Let 'em fatten up a few more days and we'll have a fish fry."

"Sounds good to me," answered Shane, "Help me look for some wild onions to put with those trout your gonna catch."

They rode down off the mountain and then north along the Arkansas River a few miles into the small town of Granite. There was a general store, post office, several houses, and the livery stable, which doubled as the stagecoach station.

There was also a church and restaurant that overlooked the river. Rows of saloons and boarding houses lined both sides of the single dirt road that led through town and followed the river north to Leadville. Granite was another wild mining town with little use for law and order.

Life pulsed with the coming and going of miners and other folks seeking adventure. Days were spent working the sluice boxes and Long Toms. Nights were spent drinking, gambling and fighting.

Steve and Shane pulled up in front of the general store, dismounted, and went inside. A big burly man with full beard and a leather apron was sweeping the floor. He looked up from his task and immediately smiled as he recognized Steve.

"Well, howdy stranger, ain't seen ya fer many moons," he said in a friendly voice as he extended a huge, meaty hand.

Steve shook his hand and replied, "Good to see ya agin', Moe. How ya been?"

"Still got that arrowhead buried in muh hip, but it don't bother me much. Ma, come in here, it's Steve," he yelled to the back of the store and a short, thin woman appeared.

"Hello, Steve," Betty said, and gave him a hug. "Good to see ya, who's the good lookin' feller with ya?"

"Oh, durn near forgot, this here is Shane McQuaid. He spent the winter with me up on the peaks. His folks share that place north of Salida with Ben Hoier. Shane, this is Moe Maas and his wife Betty."

"Oh yeah, I know them folks," answered Moe. "Wuz through there just last week. Good people too, had supper with 'em. They talked quite a bit about you," he said as he shook Shane's hand. "They told me you went to school back east to learn to be a horse doctor."

"Yes Sir, that's true, didn't like it much back there though."

"Well, I don't blame ya none. I didn't like it back there neither. Lemme tell ya, a horse doctor could make a good livin in these parts. A man could set up shop and make more money than he knew what to do with."

"Well, I might just do that one day, but I ain't ready to settle down just yet," Shane answered.

Moe looked back at Steve and said, "What brings ya down here?"

"Needin' a new shooter," he said.

"What happened to yer Hawken?" asked Moe.

"Had a slight disagreement with a griz and it got busted up," Steve answered. "Busted ma good knife too, and danged near busted ma laig.

Cut my horse up some and gouged my shoulder a bit, but he paid dearly fer that. Shane here filled 'im full o' lead and he died in or rather ON muh lap!"

"Sounds like ya had a close call. Shor glad yer friend wuz with ya. Come on back here and take a look at what I got."

They all walked to the back of the store where Moe kept an ample supply of guns. Steve looked over the selection and was interested in one that resembled Shane's gun.

While Steve looked at the rifles, Shane went over to talk to Betty.

"Do you have a Bible fer sale," Shane quietly asked.

"We sure do. Come over here."

Shane found just what he was looking for. A black, leather bound Bible with study notes. "Steve and I plan to have a bite to eat up the street. Do you think you could write his name on the dedication page real purty fer me?"

"I would be happy to and I'll wrap it in brown paper; then give it to you when you're ready to leave."

"Much obliged fer that Ma'am, thank you."

"What kinda shooter ya be lookin fer, Steve?" asked Moe.

"Need one that shoots more'n once," Steve said as he examined the rifle closely, bringing it to his shoulder and working the lever action to get the feel of it.

"If yer lookin' fer sumthin' that shoots a whole buncha times; looky here at this'n. Just got it in a few days ago. A Winchester 15 shot repeater; 44 caliber. A real beaut. Here, take a look."

Steve's eyes lit up when he saw this magnificent firearm. Its stock and forearm piece was polished walnut, the barrel was octagon.

Moe handed him a pistol he called a Colt 44 and said, "This shoots the same bullets as the rifle yer holdin'. No more pourin' powder down the barrel while a griz is chewin' on yer laig. With these two, ya can shoot a score afore ya gotta' stop and reload."

"I'll take 'em," said Steve. "What'll it cost me fer the pair?"

"What ya got ta trade?"

Steve dumped the contents of his leather bag onto the wooden counter. There were bear claws, elk teeth, and gold nuggets and ivory buglers inside.

Moe took several claws, all the ivory, six gold nuggets and asked, "Fair enuff?"

Steve nodded his head and asked, "Ya got any bullets fer these things?"

Moe took two more small nuggets and gave him four boxes of bullets.

Steve gave him two more nuggets and asked for four more boxes.

"Don't know when I'll git back through here agin', best git enuff to last a while."

Before they left, Shane traded two pistols and holsters he had gotten from the two would-be robbers, for a Winchester just like Steve's and six boxes of shells.

Both men were beside themselves with excitement over their new toys. So excited in fact that Steve almost forgot about replacing his knife. Moe reminded him by saying, "Didn't ya say that ya lost yer knife when it got busted er sumthin?"

"As a matter of fact I did," answered Steve almost in a daze as he continued to marvel at his new rifle.

"I keep my knives over here," Moe said as he led Steve by the arm over to another wooden counter filled with many knives.

Steve gained his senses back as he gazed upon the dazzling selection of cutlery.

"Here lemme hold yer shooter while ya take a gander at these," offered Moe.

Steve looked carefully over the knives, checking the handle and blade of many before he picked one that suited him. He emptied his leather bag once again and told Moe to take whatever was fair. He took two small gold nuggets in trade.

Steve pointed to the door and said, "Hay, y'all gotta come look at ma horse."

"Yer horse, why, ya git a new one?"

"Nope, just come look, you ain't gonna believe this."

With that, they all ventured out to look at Steve's paint.

"Well," Moe said, "she sure is a fine horse but I already knowed that."

"Ya see that?" Steve shouted, pointing to the mare's left flank. "Would ya say this side looks jest like the other side?"

"Well, yeah. What ya gittin' at, Steve?"

With the biggest grin Shane had ever seen on Steve's face, he watched as Steve patted his mare's left flank.

"That my friend, is where God Almighty healed ma horse!"

"Ya don't say." Moe said with a strange look on his face.

"I do say! That griz I told ya bout, swiped this here rump with his claws leavin' four deep gashes that Shane had to sew up. Now that happened jest tha other day!"

"I don't see any gashes," Betty said looking closely at the paint.

"That's cuz I prayed and God Almighty done healed her up right afore our very eyes! We both saw it, didn't we pard?"

"That's right, Steve."

"Wow! I shore would have liked ta have seen that," Moe shouted.

"Me to," said Betty.

"Hay! Guess what else happened, I done went and got myself saved."

"Oh, Praise the Lord," said Moe, "Thank You, Jesus. I've been praying for you Steve ever since we met."

"Well, it fine-a-lee took hold. Sure prechate yer prayers."

Moe slapped Steve on the back and said, "Ya won't regret yer decision, my friend."

"Well, pard, we best git some vittles afore we head out. Moe, we'll leave our stuff here and load up on our way back."

Steve and Shane ambled on down to the restaurant that was next to the hotel. They both ordered steak, potatoes, a loaf of bread, and washed it down with a pot of coffee. The meal was not bad but the beefsteaks were just not as tender and flavorful as fresh venison. When they finished, they went back to Moe's store, picked up their new purchases, and stowed them in their saddlebags and rifle scabbards.

Betty slipped Shane the wrapped Bible, which he hid in his saddlebag; then they mounted up.

"Reckon we best be gittin' back," said Steve as he leaned down and gave Betty a kiss on the forehead.

Moe shook his and Shane's hand and told them to come back to see him sooner next time. He repeated his offer about a horse doctor making lots of money and Shane thanked him and said he would keep it in mind.

They rode north out of town and then turned east onto a trail that would take them to the top of the Mosquito Range. Steve loaded his Winchester as he rode and Shane followed suit. They were constantly bringing the rifles up and taking sight on anything and everything trying to get used to the feel of the harmonious blend of hardwood and steel. They took several shots at rocks to test the guns for elevation and windage, getting to know their firearms. It was critical to know where and how your rifle shot; it could be the difference between life and death.

When they reached the crest of the ridge that led to the cabin, they stopped to let the horses rest and gaze at the beautiful landscape and watch the sunset. The dying sun was shooting orange and purple shards of light into the mottled evening sky. As far as they could see in any direction was unbroken wilderness.

"Best head fer home," suggested Steve, "afore we gotta' ride in the dark."

Shane agreed. They let the horses go at their own pace until they were on the sagebrush hill above the cabin. Then, they dismounted and walked their horses down the ridge in single file past the carcass of what was left of the grizzly, scaring a badger away from his evening meal.

It was almost dark when they arrived in front of the barn. They pulled the saddles off, gave the horses some oats, and put them up for the night. Inside, the cabin was dark, so Steve lit the lantern. Shane began to build a fire in the cook stove so he could make supper.

While Shane was engaged in fire making, Steve was admiring his new firearm. He couldn't get over the fact that it shot fifteen times before reloading. Combine that with his Colt 44 holding six more of the same bullets and it made a man believe he was in command of some powerful medicine. The only time Steve ever needed to shoot more than once was at a charging grizzly or defending himself from outlaws. He never had occasion to shoot Indians, believing that shooting the politicians would solve all the problems of the white man as well as the Indians! He was intrigued by the little metal cartridges that eliminated the need to pour powder down the barrel, then wrap a bullet in cloth and push it down on top of the powder and then put in a cap, cock the rifle, take aim, and finally shoot. All this while being chewed on or overrun by the enemy! This was a breakthrough of magnificent proportion. He could hardly wait for daybreak so he could try out his new rifle some more. He was deeply lost in thought about the unlimited possibilities of this powerful weapon when he was interrupted by Shane's voice asking him if he was ready for a cup of coffee.

"Yeah, could use a cup o' coffee, thanks," he answered. "Ya know, any man with this much firepower has got hisself some powerful medicine. It makes him equal to any critter that walks these mountains. He brought the gun to his shoulder and sighted down the barrel. "Sure is purty, ain't it?" he asked.

"Yeah, have ta admit I ain't never seen a purtier rifle," answered Shane as he dished up plates of beans and steak and shoved one across the table to Steve.

The next morning both men were up at dawn. Steve built a fire in the cook stove and Shane stepped out onto the porch into the crisp mountain air. Down in the willows along the creek he could see two cow elk and three calves. The small elk had spots on their back and had been born within the last two weeks. They were nursing as their mothers grazed on the long grass along the creek bottom. Steve came out in a few minutes and handed him a cup of coffee.

"I gotta' go to the Springs one o' these days soon," he said. "Taylor will be comin' back from Florida when school gits out and I gotta' go pick 'im up. Probly move down to the other place fer the summer.

Yer welcome to come stay with us er stay up here. Be up here agin' this fall when Taylor goes back to Florida."

Shane thought for a moment and said, "Reckon I'll stay up here. Am thinkin' I'll ride down and visit with Chief Ouray while yer in the Springs. Be there a few days and then come back up here to keep an eye on the place. May come down and visit ya from time to time, but I'm thinkin' I prefer the quiet up here."

"Well, yer welcome to stay as long as ya like," Steve reiterated. "I'll probly ride out tomorrow and move down to the other place, then just go from there to pick Taylor up."

Steve was up before dawn the next morning preparing to move to his place on Sand Creek north of Salida in the shadows of Mount Princeton. Most everything he needed was already there so it wasn't much of a move. He had the lantern lit and was building a fire in the cook stove when Shane woke up.

"What do ya want fer breakfast?" he asked Shane as he pulled on his breeches.

"Biscuits, bear meat and beans sounds good to me," Shane answered. "You make the biscuits and I'll go fetch some of that meat. Ya got the coffee made yet?"

"It'll be ready by the time ya git back from the cellar," Steve said.

Shane pulled on his boots and shirt and lit another lantern so he could see in the cellar. He walked into the dark room and set the lantern on a table. Looking around he noticed there was still an ample supply of meat that would last until fall when he would hunt again. The room was cold and made an ideal place to store meat and hides. He cut a slab of meat from one of the haunches of the bear and smelled it. It smelled fresh and would taste good with Steve's biscuits and beans.

He picked up the lantern and inspected the rest of the meat in the cellar. It was still in good shape and should keep through the summer. When he got back to the kitchen, the coffee was ready and the biscuits were in the oven. Shane put the meat on the table and began to cut it into slices. Steve poured them both a cup of coffee and sat down across from Shane to drink his.

As Shane put the meat into the skillet Steve asked, "Ya said ya wuz plannin' to go to Ouray's camp today?"

"Thought I might take a ride over there," Shane answered.

"Ya gotta' understand, it'll be a big ceremony to them people when ya ride in there. They'll stop whatever they're doin and fall all over ya tryin' to please ya. They'll be wantin' to give ya anything they think ya might need er want. Gotta be careful not to offend 'em. If'n ya don't take sumthin' they offer, it might hurt their feelin's. The chief'll dress his daughters up real purty an' have 'em on display, tryin' to entice ya into marryin' one uv 'em. It'd be powerful medicine fer him to have ya fer a son-in-law. His prestige in the tribe would soar immensely. What I'm tryin' to say is, ya won't believe the royal treatment ya'll receive when ya git there. Jest be careful not to offend 'em. They're good people, but they have tender feelins."

"Like I told ya before, I could do a lot worse than marryin' an Indian."

'Well, iffin ya do, find one that kin cook. Just be sure ya don't git saddled with one that's homey lookin, or as wide as she is tall. That kind will eat ya out of all yer vittles! Well, guess I better git movin or I'll never git outta here."

After breakfast the sun was up and washed the park with golden rays of light. The high country was alive with activity. Beaver were working in the quakies along the creek engaged in their continual effort to dam up any water that flowed. It seemed as though they just couldn't tolerate moving water and spent their waking hours working to that end. Shane watched a pair work on a medium sized aspen and presently it crashed to the ground. Steve left the cabin and headed for the barn. Shane followed along by his side.

He saddled up the paint and put everything else he wanted to take on the packhorse. He put his new rifle in the scabbard and turned to shake Shane's hand.

"Don't know when I'll see ya agin, but ya know where ya kin find me should ya crave muh company. Barrin' death or some other unnatural catasterfee, I'll see ya back here this fall."

"Hang on, I gotta gift fer ya. I'll just put it here in yer saddlebag and you can open it when ya git to yer ranch."

"Why'd ya go an do sumthin like that fer? I ain't got nutin ta give ya in return."

"Brother, you have given me more than you know. God bless you, stay safe, and don't be playin with no more bears!"

Steve laughed, mounted up, and rode off down the canyon. When he got to the edge of the timber, he turned and waved.

"See ya this fall, ride careful," Steve hollered. Shane returned the wave.

Shane led Lady into the park to graze while he prepared for his journey to visit the Utes. Not knowing exactly when he would return, he stored everything in the cellar and prepared the cabin for an extended absence. Grabbing up his rifle and saddlebags, he took one last look around and satisfied everything was ok, he stepped out onto the porch, shut, and barred the door behind him.

Walking to the barn Shane saw the bighorn grazing on the sagebrush hill. A pair of bald eagles was perched in their nest on top of a huge Ponderosa pine across the park. "Probly got younguns," he said to himself. He stopped by the shed and put all the tools into a hidie hole cache Steve had built under the dirt floor. He then took all the rest of the tack and equipment from the barn and put them into the cache as well, sealing it up, and covering it with a layer of dirt.

He saddled the mare, strapped on the saddlebags and tied on his slicker and bedroll. After his rifle was safely stowed in his scabbard, he mounted up and rode toward the top of the ridge. A powerful stench filled the air from the rotting carcass of the bear. He made a wide berth around the stinking remains. Buzzards and magpies were feasting on the remains. Shane almost gagged from the stench. He gave Lady a light nudge and soon was breathing fresh air again. On top of the sagebrush ridge, just at the edge of the timber, he stopped and took one last look at the park and the cabin. All was peaceful. He prayed that it would stay that way, and be protected from robbers, two or four legged!

The sun was high in the sky by the time Shane reached the top of the Mosquito Range. The grass grew thick and lush and waved like a green ocean in the summer breeze. Buffalo were grazing across a canyon to the east a mile away. Elk dotted the bottomland along Four-Mile Creek, their dark brown bodies clearly visible against the emerald colored meadow. Shane rode down toward the bottom of the ridge toward

Buffalo Peaks. The sky was dark blue and clouds of Clipper Ships sailed effortlessly overhead. When he reached the creek, he dismounted to drink from the clear ice-cold water. He lay down on the grass-covered bank and began to sip from the stream. The mare waded into the water to drink and in the process scared several trout that darted beneath his face and hid under the bank.

Shane stood, removed his shirt, and lay down once again and began to gently feel underneath the bank searching for the fish hiding there. When he felt a slippery body, he very carefully and slowly applied pressure around the head and tail with his hands and lifted the fish from the water. He then flipped the trout onto the bank and laid down to repeat the process until he had a half dozen fish flopping in the grass. In a few short moments he had them all cleaned and strung on a willow branch. Removing the saddlebags from the mare, he found the coffee pot and returned to the creek to fill it with water to make coffee.

Once back at the fire he set the pot on a flat rock next to the flame and searched through the bags for his skillet and coffee beans. He picked a handful of beans crushing them between two rocks and dropped them into the boiling water. He put the skillet on the fire and dropped a small portion of bear grease into it to fry the fish. When the coffee pot boiled over he removed it from the fire and set it off to the side to let the grounds settle. The fish went into the skillet next and he poured himself a cup of coffee. Leaning back against a stump, he sipped his coffee, turning the fish with his knife until they were done. He removed the skillet from the fire and scooped the fish into his tin plate. Removing the bones and tails, he flicked them aside into the underbrush and began to eat.

By the time he was finished, the sun had nearly disappeared behind the mountain, so Shane decided he would stay here till morning. He removed the saddle and blanket from his mare, letting her graze while he set about making preparations for the night. He wiped his plate with a handful of grass, which he threw into the fire, rinsed it with a little coffee, and set it on a hot rock next to the fire. He took his rifle and walked up the hill to look around before dark.

A herd of deer scattered in front of him; then stopped and peered at him from behind trees and bushes as he went by. Grouse flew up from beneath his feet and landed in nearby branches, curiously looking down at him. Shane decided one would taste good for breakfast, so he took sight on one bobbing gray head and squeezed the trigger. The headless grouse fell to the ground in a heap kicking his legs and flapping his useless wings. After a few seconds the bird lay still, Shane went over, picked it up and plucked it as he returned to camp. He removed the entrails then skewered it thru with a stiff stick, which he hung on a high limber branch. The coals glowed orange and Shane put more wood on the fire.

A mountain orchestra of coyotes serenaded the setting sun as it faded behind the black tree-lined horizon and gray columns of clouds drifted aimlessly into the purple sky. Stars began to dot the heavens and the high country began to prepare for the coming of night. Once again the fire died down to glowing embers and the last remnants of daylight were gone.

Shane moved away from the fire out into the park to lie down in the long grass and gaze up into the infinite emerald-filled black sea. The moon had not yet appeared and millions of shimmering diamonds glittered against the backdrop of cold space. A shooting star streaked across the sky in a brilliant display of exploding light creating a molten river of silver before it was swallowed up by the endless dark of night. The coyote's singing was closer now, somewhere down in the park next to the creek and getting closer all the time. Shane lay quiet in the grass as the yelping band of coyotes drew nearer and nearer. From the sound of the approaching pack it seemed they were just on the other side of the creek and coming at a fast trot. Soon they were even with Shane and he could hear them breathing as they passed by in the dark. Never suspecting his presence, they went on up the creek and he listened to their trail song as it slowly diminished, swallowed up by the distance.

The next thing Shane knew was his horse standing over him. He had fallen asleep in the grass. The moon was up and he was cold. He got up stiffly, patted Lady and said thanks for waking him up; then went back to his camp.

Poking around in the ashes he found hot coals and piling small sticks on he blew life into his dead fire. Soon he had a cheerful blaze going and warmed himself before he crawled into his bedroll for the rest of the night. He fell asleep looking across the moonlit meadow at a herd of elk.

The next morning Shane was awakened by the sound of birds singing. He looked around in the gray dawn and noticed he was in the middle of a herd of elk. Some were laying down, some were feeding, all seemed oblivious to his presence. His horse was down near the creek grazing on the dew-covered grass. Shane slowly sat up, watching the elk around him. He was surprised to find they showed little concern for his being there. They eventually moved off into the timber.

He crawled out of his bedroll and pulled on his boots. The coals still had life so he put on some kindling and blew it into a small fire. Putting on a few larger sticks, he headed to the creek with his coffee pot. As he bent to fill the pot with water, several small cutthroat trout panicked and swam under the opposite bank.

When Shane returned to camp, the fire was going strong. He put a handful of crushed coffee beans into the pot then placed it on a stone next to the flames to boil. He took the grouse from the branch and placed it in the skillet to cook. The first rays of sun were beginning to caress the top of the ridge across the park to the west. Shane leaned back against his stump to watch the morning come to life. He poured himself a cup of coffee and turned the grouse in the sizzling skillet. The flavorful aroma tickled his nose and reminded him how hungry he was. He retrieved a couple of sourdough biscuits from his saddlebags then sat down to eat breakfast.

Far across the park, quick movement caught his eye. He looked up to see a mountain lion run across a small clearing and disappear into a patch of aspen. He watched for quite some time, but the lion never came into view again. Beautiful animal, he thought to himself. A creature more silent and elusive than the wolf. Rarely heard and even more rarely seen. Sometimes at night he would sit on the cabin porch and listen to the blood-curdling scream of a lion. It caused shivers to run up and down his spine. Many times he saw where a lion had passed by the cabin in the night. The paw prints were as large as his own hands.

He finished breakfast, cleaned up his camp, and whistled for the mare. By now the sun was up and Shane was anxious to get moving. He saddled Lady, loaded his bedroll and other possibles, and rode off to the southeast from the high meadow down to the lower elevation of South Park.

It was a typical late spring morning. The park was laden with the sweet smell of sage and Shane filled his lungs with the clean, crisp, mountain air. Off to the west the crest of the Continental Divide was still covered with snow and contrasted sharply with the deep blue azure of the sky. To the east the silver tipped dome of Pikes Peak reached up to touch the sun.

The tan and white bodies of antelope seemed to be everywhere and they stood and watched curiously as horse and rider went by. A large herd of buffalo lined the horizon off to his left and he stopped the mare to study the undulating pattern they made as they grazed out of sight into one of the infinite valleys hidden in the park. It resembled the shadow of a cloud slowly moving over the ground. Quietly he rode on, his keen eyes missing nothing.

When he got to the Middle Fork of the South Platte River, he stopped for a drink in its crystal clear, ice-cold water, which a day before was on top of the range in the form of snow. The sun released it from the mother lode and sent it on its way down the mountain to nourish the land below. Cutthroat trout dashed wildly about under the hooves of Lady as they crossed to the other side. The meadow grass along the creek was filled with the sweet warbling of the Red Winged Blackbird and the complicated tune of the Meadow Lark. Prairie chickens flushed in front of them and sailed off over the sea of flowing grass and disappeared into the sagebrush several hundred yards away up on the side of the hill.

Wildlife of every description was abundant. Mink and muskrat lived all along the creek and shared the water with an occasional family of otter. Robins raised their young in the willows and a pair of golden eagles had a nest in the top of a huge dead Ponderosa pine a half mile away beyond where the prairie chickens touched down. It was peaceful and quiet here with only the sounds of the birds and the water flowing. It filled Shane with a feeling of deep serenity There was nowhere on earth he would rather be and he was happy beyond words at the beauty that was his to enjoy.

He rode till just before sundown and made camp along a small creek about four miles northwest of Black Mountain. An old prospector had built a small cabin here years ago and had since abandoned it. He took the saddle off the mare and built a fire. The mare moved off toward the creek and began to graze on the long succulent grass. Shane took his shooter and went to fetch some supper. Presently he returned with a young turkey he had sneaked up on and neatly took the head off with one shot from his pistol.

After a few minutes he had it prepared to cook. From the breast he cut strips skewered them on sturdy limbs that he placed around the perimeter of the fire. The rest he wrapped in leaves and placed in a shallow hole and covered with coals from the fire. This would be his food for the next couple days. It would cook slowly during the night.

Shane filled his coffee pot with water and put a small handful of mashed beans in and set it on the fire to boil. The sun had gone down and the air took on a sudden chill. Shane walked away from the fire into the dusk and peered up toward the heavens. A few stars were visible and off to the west arrows of orange light mingled with the mottled steel gray of the evening sky. A thin ribbon of clouds hung low over the horizon and gave the perception of a silver eel swimming into the darkness of space.

Overhead a v-shaped formation of geese flew north to their summer nesting grounds. Occasionally Shane could hear their haunting and forlorn call. He watched them for a long time until they disappeared into the night. "How can they fly in the dark," he asked out loud to himself. "Do you fly all night long?" he called after they were no longer in sight. This puzzled him. After some thought he figured they must fly until they came to a body of water that they could probably see easily from the air and then they landed. "They couldn't possibly fly all night long," he said to himself and returned to camp to find his coffee boiling over. He poured a cup of very strong coffee and sat his skillet on the fire to cook the turkey. A wolf howled from somewhere to the east and then all was quiet except for the crackling of his fire.

Presently his supper was ready, he fetched two more sourdough biscuits from his saddlebag and leaned back against a fallen tree to eat. It was now pitch black and the embers glowed red barely able to hold back the encroaching darkness Shane finished eating and walked out to where the mare was grazing. He took some oats from his jacket pocket and offered them to her. She eagerly accepted the reward as he rubbed her forehead. Overhead the stars were out in numbers and the white phosphorus river that was the Milky Way was magnificent. The moon was absent this night and these white crystals sparkled with such brilliance it threatened to overwhelm the senses. He wondered how so much beauty could be in just two colors – black and white.

It wasn't so much what was there but more of what wasn't there that inspired him. It implied emptiness and unspeakable loneliness and the ultimate definition of infinity. It was solitude and purity and dimension without limit because it had no beginning and no end. There was no way to measure it and therefore no way to comprehend its magnitude. Shane laid down on his bedroll and just stared out into the cold sky spellbound by the awesome spectacle of it all. His mind was flooded with a thousand thoughts and emotions as he searched for answers but only came up with more questions. In his subconscious he heard the nightly serenade of the song dogs and then the howl of the wolf once more....and then silence ....and he was gone to the land of dreams.

He dreamed of wondrous things; chariots of fire streaking across the heavens, horses with wings that flew among the planets and drank from the great snowy river whose water sparkled with an iridescent shimmer. He dreamed of eagles with feathers of silver that glittered, sparkled and cast an ivory shadow upon the dark ground. He saw faces of the great bears from patterns in the stars and enormous herds of pure white buffalo stampeding with only the sound of the wind to accompany them. The Lord came to him and Shane heard deep within his spirit his Heavenly Father's words.

"My son, this is your Heavenly Father; I desire to use you in ways you yet know not of. I desire for you to be immersed in and anointed with My Spirit. What you seek is within your grasp. Read the second chapter of Acts and first John. Just ask of Me to fill you with an increased measure of My Spirit and I will do it. I desire to use your life to touch others. Remember my Son's story of the talents given to three servants? I expect you to use what you have been given wisely, not for your own personal gain or benefit but to reap dividends for My Glory."

"You will begin to know My voice even clearer, but be careful. Test what you hear, believe not every spirit but those that confess that Jesus Christ came in the flesh as it is written in first John, chapter four. Those spirits that cannot answer this are not of Me. As you listen to My voice and are quick to be obedient, you will grow in wisdom and understanding. Yes, Jesus came in the flesh and has risen in glory!"

Shane awoke the next morning before sun up. It was cold and the ground was covered with dew. He rolled out of his bed stretching to get the kinks out. The fire was out except for a few coals so he stirred them up, added some kindling and went to the creek for water. The ever-present native trout scattered and hid under the bank.

"Seems like every piece of water has these fish in it," he said to himself. "Must be a jillion of 'em. Purty little critters, too, spotted with purple and red and yellow and white. Sure make a fine meal. Thank you Lord."

As he thought these words, he remembered his dream and hearing God's voice. He purposed in his heart to think on what he had heard as he rode to Ouray's camp.

The fire was going when he returned so he made coffee and dug up his turkey from the shallow pit. It was steamy hot and delicious. He took his last two biscuits from the saddlebag, put them on his tin plate and covered them with part of the turkey. Into the saddlebag went the rest of the turkey. He sat down next to a fallen tree and ate a hearty breakfast followed by a hot cup of coffee. He figured to find the Ute village sometime by late afternoon.

While he was working on his second cup of coffee, a rider appeared on the hill to the west. He was coming toward Shane in a slow manner carefully guiding his horse over the rocks and deadfall. Shane already had his hand close to his revolver, just in case

When he was within earshot, he stopped and asked, "Ya got any coffee?"

"You bet," Shane offered. "Come on in and make yourself ta home."

"Much obliged," said the stranger. "Name's Koch, Kenneth Koch. Headin' up ta Wyomin' territory. Spent the winter on Bear Creek trappin' beaver. Ain't many left. May hafta git into nother line o' work."

Shane poured him a cup of coffee and noticed his head and face were horribly deformed with huge scars.

"Pardon my asking friend," Shane queried, "but what happened to your face and head?"

The longhaired stranger smiled and said, "Had a slight misunderstandin' with a griz some time back. Chawed on me sumthin tarrible. So bad I wuz unable ta walk. Crawled fer several days eatin snakes, plants and bugs; some wuz eatable, sum wuzn't. The Sioux helped me or I wouldn't be here today."

They chatted over coffee for a good long while. Shane explaining he had spent the winter with Steve and was now headed for Ouray's camp. They talked a while longer and then Kenneth stood and offered his hand. Shane noticed he had huge, powerful hands covered with thick calluses and he felt the power of this man as he shook hands with him. It felt like he had a hold of a tree stump.

"Give muh regards ta Englert. Much obliged fer the coffee and conversation," he said as he mounted up and rode off.

Shane was dumbstruck by the stories the man had told him. Was as if he was listening to Steve himself talk. Seems he knew Steve from years back. They spent one winter trapping the Sangre de Cristos together. Kenneth stopped before he rode over the crest of a hill and waved.

Shane waved back and Kenneth rode out of sight. Shane was impressed with the man. He was quiet, pleasant, and possibly the strongest man he had ever shaken hands with; he certainly had the biggest hands.

"Would hate to tangle with him," Shane thought to himself.

As he rode, he wondered if the Ute would remember him and if they would welcome him to their camp. He knew there had been some difficulty with white men before and the Ute could be rather a nasty adversary when pushed. He also thought about what he had heard from the Lord earlier.

"Lord, you said, "ask to receive more of Your Spirit. So, Holy Spirit, fill me with more of what you have to give me. I'm askin for more of You in faith, cuz I don't understand all there is ta know about you yet. In Jesus name I pray, Amen."

All of a sudden Shane felt something rising up deep within himself. At first he wondered if what he had for breakfast didn't agree with him but that wasn't it. He suddenly had this over whelming urge to praise God.

He opened his mouth to do just that and began to speak. Then promptly shut up. "What in the world was that I just spoke?" he said out loud. He tried again, same thing happened. He tried again, same thing. "Lord, is this yer doin? What's goin on here?"

"Son, I have given you a new prayer and praise language. It is a heavenly language that I desire you to use frequently when speaking to Me. Don't be afraid, this is what is spoken of in My Word. Read second chapter of Acts and 1st John - 4. Remember, seek and you will find, knock, and the door will be opened."

So, for the next several hours, Shane began to speak in his new language, getting more fluent and at ease with it as he went along. "This is wonderfully strange," he thought. Lady thought so also because, with one ear back and a spring in her step, the miles flew by.

Chapter 24

UTE Encampment

By late afternoon, two days later, Shane found himself overlooking a bluff down into Badger Creek. He figured somewhere down this huge canyon the Utes had their village and he guided the mare carefully down through the rockslide until he was beside the creek. Up the canyon he noticed the beaver had built dams all over the valley floor and lush grass covered the ground everywhere there wasn't water.

This was a well-protected valley. It was several hundred feet deep and lined on both sides by nearly straight up and down granite cliffs and rockslide and dark timbered ridges. It was safe from the weather and invasion. He picked his way down the canyon along a trail made by either man or animal but at this time he was following moccasin tracks in the damp soil.

He knew he was getting close to his destination. Further he rode until he came around a bend into a huge park with quaking aspen growing all the way down from the top of the ridge to the floor of the park. Across the giant clearing was a gently sloping hill that was overgrown with bushes and an occasional Ponderosa pine. Above this was a straight up granite cliff that formed the northern boundary of the Ute valley.

The only way in was along the creek from above or below and the trails the Indians had made up the mountain to access their hunting grounds on top. Their lodges were arranged in an orderly fashion on a smaller bluff overlooking the creek. The camp took up no more than two acres of land situated here in this almost impregnable location.

Shane noticed their remuda across the creek and at the same time he heard a whoop and then dogs started barking and the village was suddenly a frenzy of activity. He dismounted and began to walk toward the village when several young braves ran out to him brandishing lances in a rather menacing way. Soon he was surrounded by angry looking Indians with painted faces and feathers dangling from their braided hair.

The Indians shoved and pushed him roughly and took his horse away and took his guns and knife, completely disarming him, cruelly pushing him toward the camp. The frenzy grew uncontrollable as they drew closer and closer to the camp and Shane began to fear for his life. His hands were pulled behind his back and tied.

"Lord, you said you would be with me and direct my paths. I know I'm in your will so I will fear not. You are in control of my life." A sudden peace came over him, he stood tall and managed to keep his composure as they pulled and pushed him into camp.

He saw they were beginning to become very excited. They tied him to a pole in the middle of the village, and then surrounded him shaking their lances and knives at him. Then, all of a sudden the village grew quiet and the crowd split apart and the great Ute leader, Chief Ouray appeared.

As soon as he saw Shane, a look of horror came over his face and he bellowed out, "Release him! He is Ahu-u-tu-pu-wit. He is brother of Tevvy-oats-at-an-tuggy-bone (Big Friend, referring to Steve), he is the one who saved our brother, Shavano. He is friend of the Ute. Open your lodges to him, he is friend."

With those few words the whole village was once again in frenzy. He was quickly untied with much apologizing. This time they were hugging him and slapping him on the back and treating him with the respect of a chief himself.

The whole village moved in close around him, wanting to touch him. He could sense they were genuinely sorry they had treated him so badly at first. They reminded him of how children acted in the presence of a candy man. They were all beside themselves trying to atone for their behavior, bowing and clasping his hands and touching his hair and offering him gifts that suddenly appeared out of nowhere. He couldn't imagine what the Chief had told them about him but it had to be some powerful medicine they felt he had. He was taken over to the Chief's lodge and was warmly welcomed by the chief's wife, Chipeta. Ouray spoke, "prepare a feast for our guest, this is cause for great celebration!"

The crowd dispersed and he and Shane and a few of the village elders entered the lodge of the Chief. All remained standing until the Chief asked Shane to sit and then everyone sat. A small fire was in the center of the lodge and they all sat around it on seats made of fur or elk hide. The sides of the lodge were covered with the trappings of a chief. Weapons on one side, a bow and arrows, war lance, and a braided leather rope next to a shield made of buffalo hide. On another side was his ceremonial bear claw vest and eagle feather headdress. Other interesting things adorned the inside of the lodge also.

Ouray then spoke, "It has been long since we spoke, welcome to our village, you will always be welcome here and will be protected from your enemies. You are free to remain with us as long as you wish. We are happy that you have come to visit with us."

Shane thought Ouray was articulate and eloquent with the white man's words. He spoke better than some white men Shane knew and he wondered about that. One day he would ask the Chief how he came to speak so well the white man's words. That would be for another day; for now he wanted to meet everyone.

The Chief started by introducing him to the group. He said, "This is Ahu-u-tu-pu-wit, his white man name is Shane. I have told the story to you many times how he saved the life of Shavano after we were attacked by the Shoshone."

He then went around the circle of men and introduced them in their Indian name. First was Guero (Light Hair), then Shavano who took the leather and ivory necklace from around his own neck and placed it around Shane's neck.

"I owe you my life," he said quietly, and then he sat down. Antero was next, then Ignacio, and finally Ka-ni-a-che, who had been struck by lightning two summers past and part of the hair was burnt off his head leaving him partly bald.

Each in turn, when he was introduced, would stand and approach Shane and extend his hand in friendship. He would then lay a small gift at Shane's feet. By the time the introductions were over, Shane was almost overwhelmed with emotion by the amount of honor and respect the elders had bestowed upon him. Steve was right when he had told him what to expect. He had no idea it would be anything like this. He was looked upon with as much awe as the Chief himself.

Shane stood and addressed the group with as much eloquence as he could muster. "Thank you for the gifts and kind words. I have always looked upon the Red Man as my brother. I know you have not always been treated with respect and honor by some of my white brothers. This is no reason we cannot be friends. I will never betray my red brothers in word or deed, nor will I ever fight against you on any battlefield. These words I promise until I go to my burial ground."

With this speech, which the chief translated, all the elders stood and said this was good. They all agreed it was strong medicine to have such a good friend among the white man.

Chief Ouray spoke next. "You are welcome into our village and lodges whenever it pleases you to visit. It will be reason for great celebration when you honor us with your presence. Let us go outside and begin this celebration."

The village had a large open courtyard surrounded by their lodges. They were made of animal hides, mostly buffalo, attached to a wooden frame. All the entrances faced the rising sun. In the center of the courtyard was a large area for dancing around a bonfire, which was just now being readied for the celebration to begin. Several other fires had been made and meat was being cooked. The women were preparing other foods as well. The children in the village gathered around Shane and acted like they had never seen a white man before.

Some appeared frightened and some of the braver ones would sneak up and touch his hand and then run away.

There were young women in the village all engaged in work of some kind. Most of the work in the village was done by them. They cooked, tanned, gathered food, firewood and hauled water, and raised the children. The men had the responsibility of defending the village, hunting and making weapons.

Shane was taken on a tour of the village. The location was a good one. All the lodges faced east so the first rays of the morning sun would warm their shelters. Behind the village to the west was a rock cliff that made invasion from that direction impossible. Across the creek to the north was a large sloping park where the remuda was kept and beyond this the ground gently sloped up to a granite rim rock that ran east and west and generally defined the northern border of the valley. Invasion from this direction was impossible as well because the rim rock was at least fifty feet tall. The only way down for miles was the path Shane had come in on. The park across the creek was at least a mile long and the village used it for horseracing and other recreation. In late summer the edge of this park was overgrown with berries.

On the other side of the village to the south was a very steep ridge thickly covered with dark timber. On top of this ridge was flat and extended for many miles to the east and south. It was wild and unexplored, for the most part, except by the Utes.

They used it for their hunting grounds as it abounded with buffalo, deer, elk, antelope, wild turkey and other game. It was marked by huge tracts of dark timber, quaking aspen, enormous meadows, deep long valleys and many streams and springs. A man could live in here and never be found.

Shane asked Ouray if they could go and ride around this wild country some day. The Chief agreed it would be a good thing to take him there soon. The entourage consisting of the Chief, the elders and Shane left the village and walked down the creek looking at the long Valley of the Badger. The grass was lush and green and beaver had many dams along the creek.

"We have lived here many summers now," said the Chief. "It is a good place to live. Everything is here for one to live forever. I hope my people can live in peace here. We ask no more than that."

Shane responded, "Oh, Great Chief, it is my prayer this will be so and I will do everything I can to help my red brothers live for eternity in the Valley of the Badger."

They crossed the creek and slowly walked back through the horses, upstream, past the village to another large meadow where the creek forked.

At the junction of the two streams rose a granite formation that resembled a huge tortoise. Appropriately named, the Indians called this "Turtle Rock of the Morning Sun." The sun rose every morning over the back of this granite reptile.

"You have chosen a good place for your people," said Shane. "It is safe from your enemies and protected from the snows of winter. Perhaps I will stay for a few moons and live with you."

The Chief was impressed by the compliment and said, "You would be welcome if you choose to do this."

The elders discussed this possibility and nodded their heads in agreement. All offered that this would be good for Man-With-Big-Medicine to live with them. There was much backslapping and hand shaking and Shane never felt so welcome anywhere in his life. With the exception of his own parents and Steve, Shane never seemed like he really belonged anywhere. Somehow he felt a strange bond and a kinship with these people. He would stay with them for a while and see how things turned out.

The group returned to the village as the sun was setting below the rim rock to the west. The fire in the middle of the courtyard was burning brightly and buffalo, deer, antelope, and turkey was being cooked over the other fires. The elders took their place with Shane in the place of honor next to the Chief and the festivities began. There was much food, dancing and singing as the whole village welcomed Shane into their midst.

Shane learned a great many things this day. He could not think of anyplace else he would rather be just now. The people welcomed him as if he was one of their own who had returned after a long absence.

The celebration lasted late into the night until the fires died down and everyone returned to their lodges to sleep. Shane slept in the Chief's lodge. He noticed all his belongings were stacked neatly against the wall. A buffalo robe was laid down for his bed.

With all the excitement, Shane had forgotten about his horse. He asked to be excused to tend to his horse, left the lodge, and went to check on her. Assuming she was with the other horses, he picked his way in the moonlit night across the creek and stood in the park across from the village. The mare came to him as he whistled. He rubbed her forehead, gave her some oats, and then returned to his bed.

Shane lived with the Indians for several weeks. It was now midsummer and he had been accepted into their society as one of their own. The novelty of his presence had worn off and he became another member of the village, but revered in a way separate even from the Chief. Shane thought they were like children, curios and honest and always they honored his presence with great respect. He grew to love them deeply and knew he would give his life for them if need be. And because of his knowledge of medicine and other things that the Ute thought to be magic, he was held in the highest esteem. He could not understand how some white men could treat the Indians so badly. This was a source of great consternation to him and he would do anything he could to right this wrong.

Shane was sought out often for advice and always welcomed and encouraged to sit on council meetings where his point of view carried great importance. His contribution to the village in terms of health and well-being was inestimable as far as they were concerned. Shane cured many maladies of the people and they virtually worshipped the ground he walked on and he always remembered to give the glory to the Lord.

One evening in early fall Shane was across from the village watching the horses. They were all grazing down the creek a short distance from him. His attention was diverted by a movement in the park above the village. A small herd of elk had entered the park to feed and he was watching these when he heard a whoop and looked back to the horses. He saw a strange rider on the back of his horse trying to escape. The rider made it only a very short distance before he was unceremoniously bucked off, hard. Shane alerted the village and ran down through the park to apprehend the unsuccessful thief. When he got to the place where the short rodeo had taken place, he found a young Shoshone writhing on the ground with a broken arm. Shortly, the whole village of warriors were there also. As they roughly jerked him to his feet, he gave a cry of intense pain. The braves were ready to cut him into little pieces. Shane intervened and bade them not to hurt the lone Indian.

"Take him to the village and do him no harm," he said.

All the Utes looked at Shane as if he had suddenly lost his mind, but they did as he directed. They tied the young brave to a pole and set a guard to watch him. Shane asked the Chief for a council meeting to decide what to do with the thief. Ouray called for a meeting with the elders and they all went to his lodge to palaver the situation. Shane asked if he might speak first and this was granted.

"The Shoshone is your enemy, this is true," he began. "You have always been at war with their people. They have killed many of you and you have killed many of them. This has brought much hardship and caused much hatred between your peoples. I believe it is time and this is an opportunity to stop the bloodshed now and forever. My recommendation is that you allow me to fix his broken arm and you return him to his people as a gesture of friendship. In this way, it is my hope you will no longer have to fear their attacks on your village when you hunt, and your women and children are here alone."

After Ouray translated, the elders discussed this at length and finally they all agreed this was strong wisdom and a good thing to do. Again, Shane's esteem increased among these brave men.

The Chief spoke, "It will be done as you have said. Bring the Shoshone to my lodge."

The elders left and shortly the young Indian was brought to him by Shavano, who spoke to him in the tongue of the Shoshone.

Shavano told the terrified young Indian what they had decided. His life was to be spared, his arm was to be fixed, and he was to be set free to return to his people with the message of hope that it would bring peace to both villages. The face of the youngster lit up when he discovered his life was to be spared. He would gladly take the message back to his chief.

Shane set his arm and the young brave stayed with the Utes for ten sleeps. He was even given a horse to ride back to his village.

When he left, he thanked Shane and gave him a bracelet. He told Shavano he would take the message to his people and hoped it would bring peace to them both. He then rode across the park, up the creek to the narrow trail to the top of the rim rock. At the top he stopped and raised his hand high before going out of sight onto the big prairie.

Chapter 25

A Wedding

There were several unmarried women in the village. One in particular had caught Shane's eye. She was a real beauty, with light skin. Shane had talked to Ouray concerning her on more than one occasion. The Chief told him they had found her almost dead in a wagon train that had been attacked by Pawnee. The Pawnee had killed everyone, burned the wagons, and stolen the horses. A Ute hunting party had come upon the horrible scene after seeing the smoke.

They found the unconscious girl underneath what was left of one of the wagons. She was taken to the village and nursed back to health. Having no family and nowhere to go, she stayed with the Utes and the Chief adopted her. She seemed perfectly happy here. She was considered to be one of the Chief's daughters and he hinted many times to Shane that she would make a fine wife. Ouray had been pressed many times by several young braves to allow her to be courted, but he resisted because of her young age and he felt it would be best if she married someone of her own kind.

Shane felt in his heart that this woman was just what he was looking for. He was allowed to take chaperoned walks with her, where they talked of many things. Her white name was Rebecca McCabe; her adopted Indian name was Sa-rap (Rainbow Woman) because of her flowing red hair.

She had moved with her family from Pennsylvania when she was twelve. They were part of a wagon train bound for Oregon when the Pawnee attacked. Her family was devout Christian, her father, a preacher. He wanted to take the word of the Lord to Oregon and set up a church there. All she could remember was that her wagon had overturned as they tried to escape and she was trapped underneath. When she woke up she was under the care of the Utes.

At first she was overwhelmed with grief and fear, but the Indians treated her well and took good care of her and eventually adopted her. She also eventually adopted them as her people and grew to be happy with them. She was now nineteen, well past when the young braves thought she should choose a husband. Ouray knew that soon he would have to make a decision as to her future.

After living with the Utes for seven years, she could not imagine being anywhere else. This was her home and meant security and happiness for her. Shane grew more fond of her as time went on until he knew he was head over heels in love and sought God's opinion on the matter.

The Lord came to him in a dream and said, "My son, this is the woman I have chosen for you. She will bring you much happiness and fulfill your life in ways unknown to you at this time. This is what I meant when I spoke to you in the city in the East as the other love of your life walked away from you. The Chief is waiting for you to ask for her hand in marriage. The People are waiting for this to happen with great anticipation. I will bless this union. Go forth and make this happen. I am much pleased with this."

Shane awoke the next morning and knew his life was about to change forever. He spoke to Ouray and as his dream had indicated, the Chief was beside himself with excitement of having Ahu-u-tu-pu-wit for his son-in-law. In his mind it would be a great honor to have a person with so much power and knowledge as a member of his own family. He readily gave his blessing to the couple and immediately called the elders together and told them of this great thing that was about to happen.

As the word spread of the elders' decision, it caused most of the village to become excited and they looked upon this as being arranged by the Great Spirit himself. Nothing of this importance had ever happened to the People before and they greatly anticipated the historic event. It would be a story told and retold and passed on from generation to generation of how a man with magnificent and magical powers was delivered to them by the Great Spirit, and how he chose the Ute as his people and then took one of them to be his wife. This was the sort of thing greatly revered and his standing in the village was enhanced even more, if that was possible.

There were a few though, namely the single braves, who did not look upon this happy occasion with as much relish as everyone else. Although Ouray was aware of this, he had to be careful how he handled the matter. The young braves felt they should have just as much of a chance as Shane to woo Sa-rap's hand in marriage. The old Chief confided this concern to Shane and asked if he might have a solution.

"Oh great Chief, you are a mighty and wise leader. When your elders seek your advice there is much wisdom in your words and council. I also serve a Great Chief who is full of wisdom and understanding, far above that of any man, be they red or white. You know Him as The Great Spirit that dwells in all things. I know him as God Almighty. It is from Him I will seek wisdom, then we will council one to another and see if God's words are true and just."

Ouray, looked at Shane, "This is a good thing you do. May the Great Spirit give us both wisdom in this matter."

Shane nodded and left the lodge to find a quiet place to pray and seek an answer to a potentially unsettling and dangerous situation. Those involved were proud warriors and an injustice, whether real or perceived, could have lasting consequences that could cause strife in the tribe and even death.

Shane crossed the creek and walked up stream to a quiet spot that Sa-rap had showed him. He whistled for Lady and smiled as she trotted to his side. He felt the need to have her calm, steady presence as he sought God's advice.

As Shane stroked Lady's neck and rubbed behind her ears, he thought about what he could do to keep peace with those braves who called him friend. He knew that if some sort of contest was devised involving strength, horsemanship, marksmanship or hunting he would probably win because he excelled in them all and then some. He knew that even if he won, there would still be hard feelings among some and he desperately wanted to avoid that. He suddenly raised his head so quickly that Lady jerked her head up as well, with ears forward, body tense. Shane patted Lady's neck, "easy girl, everything is alright, your master just needs a swift kick in his caboose!" What had startled Shane was the realization that although he had come to pray and seek God's wisdom, he had been trying to solve the problem with man's wisdom and not God's!

Shane bowed his head and prayed, "Lord, I humbly ask your forgiveness for attempting to figger this mess out on my own." As he opened his worn Bible, it fell open to the Book of Psalms.

Shane smiled as he saw that God had opened it to one of his favorites, Psalms 34. He knew it spoke of the happiness of those who trusted in God. As he read, he stopped on verse eight, "Oh, taste and see that the Lord is good; Blessed is the man who trusts in Him." Shane read on, ... verses fourteen and fifteen seemed to light up. "Depart from evil and do good, seek peace and pursue it."

"Yes Father, I understand but I don't understand!"

"My son, whom have you not considered? Who should make the choice? I have made Mine."

As the noonday sun tracked across the azure blue sky, Shane struggled to understand what he had just heard and he was making no headway. Suddenly, a hot breath upon his neck brought him out of his troubled thoughts. Looking up, he saw Lady only inches from his face, looking intently at him.

"What?" Shane asked. At that, Lady shook her head and stamped her right foot. Shane just sat there with a puzzled look on his face. "Lady, what is it? What's gone and got you worked up?"

Lady shook her head again; then gently placed her muzzle on Shane's right shoulder and left it there. Shane reached up to stroke her head, softly thinking she wanted to be petted, when suddenly, the fog that had been obscuring his spiritual eyes began to lift.

"Lady, are you trying to tell me, you picked me to be your master and that no one else would have been able to ride you?" Lady whinnied as she nodded her head. "In other words, it should be Sa-rap that is to make the choice of mates."

Lady backed up and looked intently at Shane, her ears facing forward. She then did the strangest thing - she winked!

"You are one fine horse," shouted Shane as he closed his Bible, jumped up, hugged Lady's neck, gave her a kiss, and took off running to find the Chief.

Shane located Ouray outside his lodge, sitting with his wife, Chipeta. As he slowed to a walk and stopped a respectful distance away so as not to interrupt or eavesdrop, the couple looked up and Ouray motioned for Shane to approach.

"I see you have an answer from your God Almighty," said the Chief.

"How did he know that," thought Shane.

"I have, but it will need your wisdom also." The old Chief smiled at this show of respect, as did his wife.

"I believe God Almighty has said we should allow Sa-rap to choose her husband in her own way. That this would preserve peace and not lessen the dignity or honor of your young men."

The Chief looked intently at Shane then closed his eyes and lapsed into deep thought. Shane knew from past experience this might take a while, so he sat cross-legged and began to pray silently. After what seem like hours to Shane but was really only minutes, the Chief opened his eyes and again looked intently at Shane. He did this for some moments then turned and looked at Chipeta.

Shane thought he saw a questioning look on Ouray's weathered face, as he looked deep into Chipeta's eyes. His wife looked back at her Chief, tears welling up in her eyes as she smiled and placed her hand on his. Ouray also smiled, nodded his head and stood.

"I must call a counsel of the elders. This that you have proposed has never been done before. We must smoke on this, but I think you have heard good wisdom and my people must learn from the One that speaks truth, wisdom and of honor among brothers."

The elders gathered in Chief Ouray's lodge that evening. The Chief asked that Shane remain outside until called. The elders were surprised that Shane was not included, but out of respect for their chief said nothing.

When all were seated, the Chief related everything that had transpired between Shane, himself and Shane's word from his God Almighty. Each one already knew of the affection the young couple had for each other and it quickly became clear why this meeting had been called.

As the night wore on, Shane prayed that God would somehow speak to these men. The rest of the village knew that something of great importance was occurring and that it concerned Shane. There was a hush over the entire camp, with the only sounds coming from the night and the low murmur of talk inside the Chief's tent.

Just as Shane was about to despair of having any future with Sarap, the Chief and his counsel exited from his lodge. Each face was unreadable, except for Shavano, who winked at Shane, something Shane had taught him to do, which Shavano was prone to do at odd and various times, much to the amusement of his friends.

As the other elders left to return to their own lodges, the Chief walked up to Shane.

"Let us walk in the light of the moon together and talk of this matter." Shane walked beside Chief Ouray in silence waiting for him to speak first.

"We have talked many words. Some did not want to break with tradition and tribal custom. Another wanted a contest to see who was most worthy to marry the Chief's daughter. This argument was quickly silenced, as all knew there was none more worthy than you. All voices were heard and each opinion discussed. Then one who is respected and has much wisdom stood to speak. He reminded us of many things about his white brother. How he had worked long to care for and heal our people of sicknesses. How you never lost your temper, but treated all with fairness and justice. He said many more things but the last of his words were words that could not be denied. We smoked two pipes and all agreed that your God Almighty has great wisdom and desires only peace and honor for my people. I desire to know more about the one you call God Almighty. I will tell Sa-rap that she may deal with choosing a husband in her own way.

Shane fought to keep the tears of joy from flowing. It didn't work; he could not hold back what he was feeling in his heart. The old Chief looked and softly said, "This is good medicine."

Sa-rap, upon learning of the council's decision went to each brave she knew desired her hand in marriage. With tenderness, grace, and the help of the Lord, she succeeded in strengthening bonds of friendship and causing each to look upon her as their little sister.

When Sa-rap told Shane what happened, he thanked God for giving him such a wonderful life mate. The two were married with great ceremony and celebration that lasted for days. There was much excitement and the people considered this to be the single most important event in their history to date. Shane was thought by many in the village to be a spirit in his own right and the thought that he had selected one of their own to be his mate was almost beyond their comprehension. This was most certainly a match arranged by divine intervention and the people felt great joy to be a part of such a monumental and historic event. They all felt this match strengthened the entire village.

It was many days before the excitement died down enough for the couple to have some time to themselves, for this was not just an event for the two of them but for the whole of The People as well.

When they were finally alone, they became as one in body and soul and their spirits united for eternity; one life, one voice, one heart, one mind for as long as the wind blows and the grass grows; until their dust be washed away by the rivers of time.

Shane was fond of looking into her emerald green eyes, becoming lost in their depth. He could read a story there that had gone untold until now. There was great promise and intelligence and respect for things he held dear.

She loved the wilderness as much as he did. There was hope, and fire, and strength. There was passion beyond anything he had ever known before. Her mouth tasted like wild strawberries and her voice sounded like the music of flowing spring water. Her hair was red like

Aspen leaves in the fall and her skin was smooth like drifted snow. This beautiful creature gave Shane a dimension to his life he could not have foreseen; her love made him whole; his love made her even more beautiful. This union had been arranged by God before either was born. It simply took the eternity of time to happen.

As days passed, they became so close they could communicate almost without talking. He knew what she was thinking and she knew what he was thinking. They shared their love for the wilderness that surrounded them and they spent a lot of time there; they became inseparable. She taught him everything she learned being an Indian and he taught her everything he learned being a white man. They used this to benefit the people in the village and it became their world. All thoughts of anything outside diminished. All they needed was here.

They were devoted to each other and to the tribe. The Chief looked upon this and discussed it with the elders. They agreed it was a good thing and the village had grown strong as a result.

The days were growing colder and the quaking Aspen began to take on their wild and brilliant autumn hues. It was time to fill the larders with meat for the coming winter. The night before the big hunt a vicious thunderstorm made the heavens alive with fire and the ground tremble with the roar of a thousand cannons. The village was drenched. All night long the merciless rain pounded the land of the Ute.

As the storm unleashed its fury, Shane and Sa-rap were unaware of the lighting and thunder. In fact, they were thankful for it. From then on, it was their secret joke when his wife would smile and casually say, "Sure wish it would rain."

With morning, the sun came bringing sweet smells and only the cloud nests on jagged rim rock gave hint of the violent storm. The men would leave the village this day and go to the hunting grounds to the south. Meat, from the buffalo they took, would be brought back to the village from time to time during the hunt until a sufficient quantity was obtained to last through the winter. The hunt might last for one or two days or it could last for a week.

It depended on how quickly they found the buffalo and how far from the village they were when they found them. The women would cut, dry the meat and tan the hides, which were used for clothing, repair of lodges, ropes, snowshoes and many other things vital to the tribe. The hunt was blessed, for many buffalo were killed and the useable parts were brought back to the village.

When they returned, the hunters were greeted with great ceremony. This was one of the most important events of their lives, as it assured they would not go hungry this winter.

The meat was carefully unwrapped and some of the women immediately began the task of preparing it for the feast that would follow. Other women took the hides and stretched them on racks to tan. There were endless uses for the skins of animals and the buffalo was the most important.

Great cooking fires were started and much feasting and celebration took place. For two nights drums throbbed as the feet of the dancing braves thumped and beat upon the age old Valley of the Badger. The reed flutes, rattles and wailing chants of the musicians and vocalists pierced the dappled sky with the plaintive recount of mighty deeds during the hunt.

For the next two weeks, the women worked hard preparing the meat and tanning the hides. Rack after rack of drying meat stretched from one end of the camp to the other. Many buffalo intestines filled with pemmican and sausage hung from branches throughout the village. The new hides were used to repair lodges and many feet donned new moccasins.

Sa-rap made Shane a pair of breeches and a shirt. All members of the village benefited from the hunt. This was the time of the Red Man's Christmas.

Spring came earlier than usual to the Valley of the Badger. The ice broke and great walls of muddy water raged down past the village cutting the people off from their horses for several days. The sun grew stronger and meadows shown with flowers and new grass. Light green color appeared in the naked branches of the Aspen and soon they were in full summer dress. By the time the last snows disappeared from the shadows of the great timbered ridge, the land was alive with the rebirth of a new year.

Early one afternoon the village was alerted,. A sentinel, watching the horses and the village, looked upon the hill across the park to see several Indians riding single file toward them along the base of the rockslide. They were Shoshone, but not dressed in war paint. They rode through the park until they were across from the village lined up abreast of each other. Shane recognized the young brave who had tried to steal his mare.

There were a dozen Shoshone and an empty horse. The visitors appeared to have no weapons and seemed to want to engage in big talk with the Ute leaders. They dismounted and walked a short distance down the creek and summoned the Utes for a palaver.

Chief Ouray gathered his elders and crossed the creek to meet with the Shoshone. Washaki, Chief of the Shoshone, greeted Ouray with a friendly gesture and started the conversation by thanking him for sparing his son. He welcomed this as a chance to make lasting peace with the Ute who had been their enemies for many seasons. He recounted how many lives had been lost on both sides because of hostilities that had gone back for so many winters that he had forgotten why they were even enemies. He brought a horse to replace the one they gave his son. Washaki asked about the great white medicine man that had cared for his son and Shane was summoned. He presented him with a prized bear claw necklace and thanked him humbly for helping his son and showing mercy when perhaps no one else would have, considering the circumstances. From this time on the Ute would be friends of the Shoshone. Never again would blood of a Ute be shed at the hand of a Shoshone and the Ute and Shane would be forever welcome in his village.

Washaki took a long pipe from a ceremonial blanket, unwrapping it carefully, and asking Ouray if he would share a big smoke of the sacred pipe with them. Ouray assembled his chiefs in a semicircle and Washaki did the same. He insisted that the great white medicine man stand next to him in the position of honor. He filled the sacred bowl with special tobacco and lifted it to the heavens. After speaking some words, Shane did not understand, he took a long pull on the pipe, exhaled, and passed it to him. Shane drew a puff into his lungs and passed it to his left. This went on until all had partaken of the sacred smoke. Washaki then, carefully wrapped the pipe in its special blanket. He and the rest of the Shoshone returned to their horses and mounted up.

"It is good that the Ute and the Shoshone are no longer enemies." He raised his hand in a salute to peace and led his warriors out of the Valley of the Badger.

All the people of the village had lined up along the bluff overlooking the park where their chiefs had sat and smoked with their long time enemy. They could not hear the words that were spoken but because the sacred pipe had been passed among the Chiefs of both tribes it must be big medicine. The elders crossed the creek back to the village and walked among their people telling them that the Shoshone were no longer their enemy.

For generations, the Shoshone had been hated and feared by the Ute. Many times they had come in the night and stolen horses, and many times people were killed. Without exception, the Ute would retaliate and more people were killed.

And so it went, back and forth down through history, each tribe trying to get back what it had lost from the other; trying to get even and both losing more and more as time continued until the score was forgotten and the reason for fighting was lost in the passage of time. Not one from either side knew how or when it started, only that it must continue for some reason that was also unknown. It was something that had always been and would always be and the reason was unimportant. No one had thought to ask why they were enemies and now suddenly it was all over. There was peace at last in the Valley of the Badger and a great happiness settled over the village all because of Shane.

The days had come and gone until it was now midsummer. Shane grew restless and felt confined within the granite walls of Badger Creek. His blood was yearning to explore, to go places he had never been. He wanted to take his wife and ride all over the countryside and see what was there. His mind was on a cabin somewhere high up on the slopes of the Rockies far from civilization. The Utes had taught him a great many things and they had learned much from him as well. So, he prayed and listened. Shane then talked to Sa-rap about leaving the Valley of the Ute.

"My place is with you," she said, "I will follow you to the ends of the earth."

Shane went to Ouray, told him of his decision and asked for a palaver with the elders.

The old leader assembled his chiefs, telling them their great white brother wished to speak to them. They gathered in the lodge of Ouray in anticipation of whatever words he had this day.

"My life with you has been good," he began, "I have much enjoyed your friendship. The Utes have been my family. I will always consider you to be my brothers. My time with you is short; my heart tells me it is time to leave. I know not where the Spirit will guide me, but in my heart I will always be close to the people who welcomed me into their wickiups, gave me a wife, and accepted me as one of their own. I have learned much from you, things I could not learn on my own. I have soared as the eagle with you and shared in the passage of time. We have walked together in the path of light and become as one. We have chased the buffalo and shared in the feast; we have shared each other's fires and talked of many wondrous things.

You have listened as I have told you about my God Almighty. You have pondered His words that I have shared with you. In doing so, you have shown me great honor and respect. My heart grows heavy with the thought of leaving you, but I am reminded of the memories that I take with me as I leave the great valley of stone. I need only to gaze at the full moon and know that my people are looking at the same moon and that we share the same vision. We shall depart after two sleeps."

After these words, Shane sat down. No one spoke. Eventually, Ouray stood to speak. "Those were good words for my ears to hear. There has been much time passed since I heard such words. They are spoken by a man with great wisdom who has given much to our people. Our hearts are sad that you must leave but we understand. You will always be welcome in our village, we hope you come this way often Tevvy-oats-at-an-tuggy-bone."

Shane had only heard Ouray refer to Steve by that name and he realized that he was now respected as much as Steve was by the Ute Indians. His heart swelled with pride. Ouray took the ornate ceremonial pipe, filled it with sacred tobacco, and said, "Let us smoke the pipe of peace in honor of our great white brother." He stood and offered it to the heavens, made a silent chant and lit the bowl. He inhaled deeply, filling his lungs with the sweet smelling charge. Slowly and with great ceremony he blew it outward from his lips and after the proper interval passed the pipe to Shane. After each elder had partaken and the pipe returned to Ouray, he stood and knocked the bowl clean. After refilling it a second time he said, "We have been much honored by your passage of time with us. Such a thing should be remembered with a second passing of the pipe of peace. It may be many moons before we share the big smoke again."

He offered the pipe to the heavens once again and made a silent chant. He brought fire to the charge and filled his lungs with a long draw. Exhaling with the same script as before, he passed it to the great white brother on his left.

Again it went around and the Chief said, "It is good that we have shared the sacred smoke together. May the Spirit guide you and be with you in your travels." For the next two hours the men stayed in the lodge of the chief and spoke of many things. As the meeting ended, the elders left silently, engrossed in their own thoughts; all but Shavano who, with wet eyes, hugged his brother, looked into his eyes then turned and hurried out, not trusting himself to speak.

It was night by the time the meeting broke up, the village brightened by only the light of a full moon. Shane could see the horses across the creek grazing in the long grass. He went to his lodge and found Sa-rap waiting for him. She stood and embraced her husband and ask that he accompany her on a walk in the shallow night. She took his hand and led him out into the main courtyard. They walked past other lodges, down the sloping bank, and across the shallow creek. As they walked past the horse, Lady spotted them and trotted over. Sa-rap reached up and stroked Lady's forehead and was surprised when the giant mare lowered her head, placing her muzzle on Sa-rap's right shoulder.

"With that, Sa-rap kissed Lady on the forehead and took off running down the long park, eventually stopping alongside the sparkling water at the first of many small beaver ponds. Shane caught up with her, tackling her, causing both to fall, rolling in the soft grass laughing.

Shane laid back looking up into the face of his beautiful wife as she leaned over him. He touched her smooth skin with the back of his fingers and stroked her long red hair as it cascaded around her face. She had decided earlier in the day not to braid her hair for she knew her husband liked it just as it was now. She kissed him, then laid down beside him with her head on his broad chest.

"All is well, the elders are in agreement," Shane told her. "They are sad, as I am, but understand our need to move on and follow my God and His plan for us."

Sa-rap was uncertain why they had to leave, but knew she would follow her husband wherever he went and be his partner in all things.

They lay together until the moon disappeared, leaving them in darkness with only the stars for light. Sa-rap stood and beckoned Shane to return to the village with her. Slowly he got to his feet, pulled her close and kissed her. Hand in hand, they then walked back to their lodge.

The village was up with the sun the next morning. Women were starting cooking fires, and the men were checking the horses or repairing their weapons or just sitting around talking. Shane and Sa-rap were preparing for their departure with the next sunrise.

Shane had tried to trade a rifle to Ouray for a pony to use as a pack animal, but the Chief would have none of it. Instead, he told Shane to pick whatever horse he wanted and it was his. Shane got the impression that Ouray would have been insulted if he refused the gift.

Shane selected a horse that was sturdy and would make a good pack animal. Actually, it was Lady who helped pick the horse, much to Shane's amusement.

He then made necessary attachments to load everything on the horse without having to use a travois. He figured out a way to balance their possessions in two bags made of buffalo hide and then hang them from a wooden frame on either side of the horse. Everything they owned could be carried in this manner without the worry of hanging up a travois in thick timber or deadfall. By sundown all their possessions were ready to be loaded. A final celebration was scheduled this night to bid the couple farewell.

The village assembled in the courtyard around the huge bonfire. The great Ute Chief stood to speak and the village grew quiet. "Oh Great Spirit, guide these two on their journey as they depart the Valley of the Badger. Walk with them and protect them from their enemies. May their bellies always be full and their bed protected from the cold wind. Help them find their way back to this village where they will always be welcome. It is our hope that they return often."

Ouray finished his prayer then spoke directly to Shane. "Our Great White Brother, you have been sent to us by the Spirit Himself to strengthen the people of the Ute Nation. We have grown stronger with your guidance and big medicine. It is your wisdom that gave us peace with our enemy the Shoshone. You have cured much sickness in our village and this gives us much happiness. Your worth to my people has been as the water we drink and the air we breathe. The sunrise will bring a sadness in our hearts and an emptiness in our village that will never pass. Your name will be spoken with hushed voices and the legend of your magic will be passed from generation to generation. You will be forever in our hearts from this day forward. A monument to your greatness will be painted beneath the Turtle-Rock-of-the-Morning-Sun to honor your passage of time with us. Your presence will be felt long in the valley of stone Tevvy-oats-at-an-tuggy-bone."

Shane felt a twinge in his chest as these last words were spoken and his eyes filled with tears. Never had he felt so overwhelmed with words spoken by a human being. Never had he been so touched by the eloquence of a few simple expressions. He did not trust his voice and could not speak. The elders gathered around hugging him and placing their hands on his shoulders and the women and children reached through the crowd to touch his hands. Tears streamed down the cheeks of all the women and the village was solemn and quiet.

Even the elders were at a loss for words just now. Shavano attempted to speak but his voice broke and he could not continue. Shane turned to embrace his wife and tears ran uncontrollably down their faces. After many minutes, the village regained its composure and the celebration could continue. There was much dancing and singing and merriment to honor their last night in the village despite the great sadness that was felt. The moon was straight overhead when the big fire died down and the village went to sleep.

The next morning when Shane and Sa-rap awoke, the entire village was outside their lodge waiting. As soon as they stepped into the crowd all the women broke down into uncontrollable tears and Sa-rap took turns hugging her sisters.

Shavano helped Shane tie the bags to the packhorse and attached a riding blanket to Sa-rap's mount. Shane saddled Lady, put his rifle, bedroll, and saddlebags on. His 44 Colt strapped and tied down on his hip. They were ready. The village formed two lines through the courtyard that ended in front of the Chief's lodge.

The two walked between the lines of people touching them and saying their good byes as they went, until they stood before the lodge of the Chief. The great Ute Chief stepped into the courtyard in full ceremonial dress.

Shane had never seen him dressed like this before. He was resplendent in full eagle headdress, white elk breeches and matching shirt decorated with ivory and porcupine quills. His long hair was braided and hung down in front of his breastplate and he carried a curved war lance. He walked over to Shane and offered him his hand.

"Our Great White Brother has been like a son to me. I could not love my own son more. May the Great Spirit walk with you and protect you in this life. May we meet in a future life in the land of many lodges Tevvy-oats-at-an-tuggy-bone."

With these words he placed both hands on Shane's shoulders and said good-bye. Sa-rap embraced the old chief and with tears in her eyes, she sobbed her final farewell.

Shane shook hands with the other elders and Shavano hugged him tightly. With tears in his eyes, he said good-bye to the man who had saved his life and become his blood brother and friend.

"Return to our village soon my brother. May the Spirit guide and protect you until we meet again," it was all he could say as his voice broke and he could speak no more.

Shane and Sa-rap mounted up as many hands reached out to touch them a final time. They looked down into sad faces, with tear-stained cheeks, as they rode to the edge of the camp, surrounded by the whole village.

Slowly they guided the horses down the gentle slope toward the creek accompanied by the rhythmic sound of stamping feet and clapping hands.

Just before entering the trees they turned to wave and a thunderous tumult with hands thrust to the sky exploded from the village. One final outpouring of emotion and the couple was out of sight riding up the trail through the thick timber. It was a good long while before they could no longer hear the voices of their people. They rode in silence the rest of the way to the top of the ridge and broke out into the large park. Shane stopped his horse and Sa-rap rode up beside him.

"I will miss my people," she said, but I would miss you more. I am proud to have you for my husband and my place is beside you, wherever that may take us."

"I hope we can return and visit them often," Shane answered as he looked deep into her green eyes." They are my people as well and I will miss them as you do. But right now, I want to show you God's handiwork and let you see The Master's touch. It is even more beautiful than the Valley of the Badger."

As Shane and Sa-rap headed south they were not yet aware of the plans God had for their lives. Even as they headed home, Shane could not shake a nagging feeling that something was not right.

Not many miles away there were men slowly and systematically searching for anyone who may have heard about or seen the horse Shane now rode and there were plenty who had. The Syndicate had stationed men in every town along the Front Range and the Upper Arkansas River with the promise of a fat reward for information leading to the return of their investment.

END OF BOOK ONE

Look for the exciting continuation of the Shane McQuaid Series coming soon.

Book Two is loaded with romance, two becoming one, humor, danger, suspense and a race for life.

For comments and info. contact:
Bruce: coldsky@wildblue.net
Jim: coldsky@earthlink.net

May our Lord Bless You Daily

About the Authors

<u>Bruce Dunavin:</u> Retired USAF Major, electrical engineer, wildlife photographer, fly fisherman, bow hunter, mountain man and hermit. Devout Christian, lives in Colorado.

<u>Jim Jennings</u>: USNR, Boy Scout & Explorer leader, outdoors man, backpacker, retired Texas oilman, Christian leader and counselor. With wife, Donna, lives in North Carolina. Married daughter and three grandchildren who constantly raid my icebox!